I0684330

NICK and the 996

A Porsche 911 Novel

The Creamy Way Galaxy - Book 1 (Series)

WRITTEN BY LEE VAUGHN

PUBLISHED BY VAUGHN LLC
FICTION SCIFI ADVENTURE

Please enjoy our audiobook read by the author:

COPYRIGHT © 2024 All Rights Reserved.

No part of this publication may be copied or reproduced in any format, by any means, electronic or otherwise, without prior written consent from the copyright owner and publisher of this book.

Chapter One

It was New Year's Eve on Earth, a lost night for the abandoned silver mining town of Red Ruby. In the stillness and serenity of the night, his thickset, black, extraterrestrial eyes were drawn to a stack of weathered brown boxes—roughly twenty or thirty—piled along the back door. They had been delivered, resting cheerlessly against the garage's gray, sun-beaten, chalky exterior.

Nick inhaled deeply as he descended in the twilight down the steps of his alien spacecraft, absorbing the dry scent of the Nevada desert. The cool winter wind stirred tiny dust devils that danced around the abandoned, decaying mechanic's garage, creating a scene imbued with an aura of forgotten history and untold stories.

As he entered the dark, dilapidated shop, the sharp, fluorescent rays of his aluminum craft filtered through the grimy windows. While his eyes adjusted to his new surroundings, he began a partial inventory spree, promptly attending to the boxes and opening a few in his excitement.

The laser glow from the spaceship refracted on the wrenches, screwdrivers, polishers, and spare parts littered around the cold, cracked cement floor and chipped workbenches. The defined sense of history in the garage walls silently cheered him on. Each tool was a familiar friend, ready to be wielded in the service of the brilliant engineer's ambitious new project.

Over the years of abandonment, the paint had peeled away inside, exposing weathered wood and rusty metal. Tumbleweeds and even small palm saplings proliferated through cracks in the foundation, giving the metallic-smelling shop a wild undertone of unkempt air mixed with the scent of motor oil.

Small mounds of kitty litter had been spaded across the floor, absorbing oil-stained spills. Dust was settled on every surface, including items that were once pristine and could still glimmer beneath their dusty layers. The space was stacked high with motorcycle components, steel muffler fragments, engine blocks, oil cans, chains, filters, and everything motor-related. A few greasy plastic buckets with fingerprints were positioned to catch the drips from the ceiling during the infrequent rain that blessed the desert.

Tools hung haphazardly on the walls, also scattering the light with their smooth but scarred surfaces. The ground was littered with other unattended oil stains and remnants of past repairs, a mechanical graveyard. Despite its deteriorating condition, the garage had a cozy feel, and endless potential, waiting for a day of resurrection.

Nick pulled a folded piece of paper from a secret pocket sewn into his custom, coffee-brown, knitted scarf. He'd patiently waited for this moment to arrive. After eyeing the perfect location, his long, slender, amphibian-like, green-glowing fingers pinned the list to a thin tack board on the wall opposite the locked metal bay doors; the act ceremonious, as if he were cementing a pact with himself. It was a set of rules he'd transferred from his home planet, Vetu, under the twin suns that bathed his world in perpetual twilight.

Transporting the Porsche back to Planet Vetu felt like one of the easier tasks, though complying with the rule about never returning to Earth again after the galactic race weighed heavily on his mind. He liked Earth and had visited on past vacations when intergalactic leisure travel was permitted to populated planets by the Multiverse Alliance. Forfeiture of the classic car carried a risk to his mission, a forced donation to the World Cars and Coffee Club of Planet Vetu.

While the rules stared back at him, Nick's thoughts drifted to how he had scoured cosmic marketplaces and holographic forums online, sifting through leads until he stumbled upon the proper Porsche—over twenty years old, another rule of the race. This quest was pivotal, merging his passions with a sense of purpose rooted deeply in Planet Vetu's culture of innovating propulsion systems.

Nick set to work in the garage as he tried to sort through years of accumulated clutter. He envisioned a location that felt like home, where he could not only work but also unwind.

Finding an old broom and dustpan, he began to clear away the dirt and debris from the main traffic areas and revealed the potential—hidden beneath the piles of chaos.

It was time to illuminate his new refuge as dusk finally settled in, so Nick uncovered two electric vehicle chargers from one of his packages. The thick, rubber-coated cords weighed down with promise. He carefully began his initial project, splicing them together and rewiring them according to his carefully crafted plan. He intended to install a transfer switch at the breaker box outside the garage and retrofit the power cords, ensuring that he could harness power from his spacecraft and solarized blue tarp.

As he stepped back, surveying his hand-drawn diagram, the pinned rules, and the array of tools, a wave of nostalgia surged through him and kickstarted his imagination, which often pulled him into other worlds. However, it was quickly disrupted by the faint grumble of approaching machinery.

The faint noise grew louder as it advanced along the lengthy, unpaved, private driveway, twisting through the small canyon, which ultimately connected to a narrow, elevated State Highway. He'd meticulously scheduled his journey from Planet Vetu, aligning it perfectly with the forecasted delivery of his Porsche 911. The moment he'd eagerly awaited was finally at hand. The stakes were higher than ever, with the race and contest drawing nearer as every second ticked in the galactic clock.

To greet the massive eighteen-wheeler that carried his Porsche in the extended, white trailer, Nick mutated into his human guise—a clean, orderly, middle-aged Caucasian man of forty years. Given the dual suns of his home planet, clothing was often optional. So, he speedily tore open a few more of his remaining packages and rummaged through the contents, successfully locating the jeans and shirts he'd purchased. But after dressing himself, he still stood barefoot on the cold, cracked concrete.

As the delivery truck crunched over the gravel and rumbled to a stop, Nick's heart raced in time with the idling engine. Half past eleven o'clock, the trailer door swayed downward, revealing the glossy silhouette of the black monster. The truck's ramp whined like a baby as the driver pressed many buttons, lowering it with grace. Once the motor turned over, the mean Carrera unleashed a beastly roar, awakening from a lengthy slumber with Zeus and the gods. It was more than a car; it was his ticket to a new life, the crucial restoration of his social standing.

As the loud growl filled the sky, Nick stared in awe. Though he'd owned a 911 years ago, it had never thundered this way, nor had any other propulsion system he'd owned. The custom Fabspeed exhaust griped as the driver shifted the beast into reverse and gently danced with the accelerator and clutch to back the car off the lift. He let it idle so Nick could perform a walk-around and assume payment for delivery.

Nick casually handed the driver a manufactured credit card linked to a deceased person's pilfered identity. "Here you go, we'll charge this on a Visa," he said confidently, pausing to admire his car.

A few moments later, "Z-cline," the truck driver said.

Nick furrowed his brow. He didn't understand. "What's that mate? S-say it one more time," he responded.

"Z-cline. Credit-car z-cline!"

"Oh, uh, a decline. Okay. Wait! Decline? Ehe, t-that's impossible! There's no way that can decline!" Nick yelled. "Let me call my buddy Azi," he said nervously.

"I take z Porsche!" The driver almost yelled, raising his tone.

"Okay, just wait!" Nick hurried inside to fetch another credit card from the secret pocket in his scarf and quickly returned. The driver reattempted and successfully processed the payment, a relief for both of them. "My apologies," Nick continued, nodding his head.

At that moment, he then courteously requested the delivery driver take a snapshot of him, handing over his slim, advanced mobile device, proudly capturing the first memory with his newly cherished coupe.

The 2003 Porsche 911 GT2 sat supreme in silhouette amidst its own snuffling chaos, a phoenix waiting to rise. Nick's intention solidified, further hardened by the silent whispers of the Mohave winds and the near promise of glory. He knew what lay ahead—days and nights of relentless work and the weight of impending secrecy hovering over his dual existence.

As the evening deepened, Nick felt the first hint of triumph—a spark that would ignite a journey through time, torque, and an unfolding tale where steel and sentiment intertwined in the dusty aisle of an old garage. Despite its aged exterior, the once-buried coupe, slightly hazed with swirl marks, gleamed joyfully like a treasure unearthed beneath the pegged stars in the blanket of outer space.

Approaching the car, his human fingers traced its smooth yet imperfect surface, a link to its past, possibly tumultuous life on the winding roads.

He unlatched the door of the widebody, inhaling the scent of the high-quality premium leather faintly tinged with age as he settled into the driver's seat. Memories washed over him— days spent in the grand arenas of Vetu, watching sleek machines fly for supremacy. The World Cars and Coffee Club had always been his sanctuary, a hub where native automotive passion and friendly rivalry intertwined.

The Galactic Auto Race—also known as the G.A.R.— was rare and more than a challenge; a race that occurred only once every hundred years, its hosts adding a unique twist to the rules for each instance, now classics. It wasn't just any run-of-the-mill race like the many local circuits he'd entered in the past. This was the racing Olympics, a rite of passage, a proving ground to display one's craftmanship and engineering prowess. It was the race of the century, broadcast throughout the galaxy, the only one he'd never had the chance to enter until now.

He was eager to drive the car right away. However, during his test drive, to his surprise, he heard disturbing clunking and rattling noises coming from underneath the vehicle—likely due to suspension issues the Miami dealer had failed to mention.

Despite the clean service records he'd reviewed and the pre-purchase inspection for which he'd paid an independent shop, a pin now pricked his bubble. He tried to assure himself it was nothing major, probably only some minor adjustments. He knew there would be obstacles, so held his spirits high and returned to secure the car in the garage for the night, the ample space with the potential to accommodate ten Porsches.

Taking several laps around the car, Nick carefully examined each section of the exterior, illuminated by his hanging garage string of lights. Still, the dimness somewhat hindered his visibility in identifying imperfections and areas needing repair. However, he noted, while his ideas and excitement for the restoration continued mounting. Despite the car's few battle scars, there was an undeniable charm, a potential waiting to be unveiled. The cluttered garage was stocked with tools—each a relic from the previous occupant's untold saga, yet promising a future of meticulously engineered excellence.

Nick leaned against the cool metal of the legendary Porsche, his mind drifting back to his previous visits to Earth. In the silent, dusty expanse of the garage, memories surfaced with vivid clarity. He could almost taste the acrid scent of burning rubber and feel the vibrations of engines roaring past. His motivation rebounded as he recalled the pure, unadulterated thrill he'd experienced watching the races at Le Mans.

Nick's mind flickered back to his first encounters with the Cars and Coffee Club on Planet Vetu—which now the regulars referred to as the WCACCV2. Before he was elected president of the auto club and before even joining the board, he'd always been captivated by the excitement of machines racing the contemporary tracks on weekends. He strongly agreed with the sense of fellowship among other enthusiasts and the contributions it brought to his community.

Races, the camaraderie along pit lanes, the hum of engines—they were soulful tunes of his existence. These memories fueled his determination, guiding him through his recent haze of fatigue and increasing loneliness. Back home, the WCACCV2 said he was washed-up, unable now to find victory in even the most straightforward of races. They referred to him as '*Old Dog.*'

Nick was adamant in his quest to triumph in the race back home, eager to demonstrate he still had the magic touch; that he wasn't an Old Dog. Every aspect on Earth was crucial, yet the preservation of time topped all.

The following day would mark his attempt to embrace the earthly New Year, now accompanied by his new icon. It would be a day dedicated to unwinding after a lengthy journey, organizing his space for a French press and hot plate, and assembling other essentials that would define his daily routine.

After the full day of travel and delivery, he began to slow his pace preparing for a night of restorative sleep. He ascended the roughly finished staircase to the loft, where the first three worn and splintered steps carried more charm and untold stories.

On the quiet morning of the New Year, Nick heard the rustling of a new vehicle. His ears distinguished the sounds of the vibrations and the engine as it made its way down the long, wavy, private drive. It wasn't an eighteen-wheeler but possibly a sizable vehicle.

Nick pulled on his crisp blue jeans and narrowed his view through a small, square window from the shadowed loft atop his garage. A brown delivery truck rolled to a stop, rock music pulsating as a driver stepped out. She hastily carried three stacked packages in her arms toward the back of the garage. She sported a brown uniform with a matching company hat, her blonde ponytail sprouted from the back, bobbing with each stride.

However, a large, blatant sign he'd newly erected immediately captured her attention. Directing with an arrow and bold letters that read, "Please deliver to the front door." The warning was essential due to the fact his spacecraft was now concealed in the rear driveway, obscured beneath the blue solar tarp.

Nick swiftly descended his loft, his clothes sagging around his gummy frame until he reached the front door of the garage and shifted into human form. Upon swinging the door open, the driver greeted him with an enthusiastic grin, a broad smile that brightened her face. "Hey there! I've got some packages for you, um, Mr. Bates?" she called out, her voice a lively melody that danced against the stillness of the garage. Nick felt a twitch of excitement, his heart performing an unfamiliar flutter at her arrival.

"Hi, who are you?" Nick greeted, awkwardly half-raising a hand. His human form still felt strange—like wearing a suit that never fully fit.

Yet the driver's feminine presence made the discomfort almost bearable. She must have been in her late twenties or early thirties, a few inches shorter than Nick, his human body six feet. She had proportionate facial features and body parts—precisely what a naturally discerning hound would consider prime mating material. However, Nick, being from a highly evolved race of beings, remained calm and friendly.

"Big Brown." She announced the company, her eyes bouncing from his bare feet and then back to his face. "You've been ordering quite a few things, haven't you?"

"Big, Brown?" Nick questioned softly, furrowing his brow.

"Um, yeah..." she answered, confused about why *he* was confused. "Like B-B," she enunciated slowly, trying again with him while clearly not wanting to reveal her name to a stranger yet.

"Oh, Bebe!" Nick exclaimed. "You can leave them here, Bee," he said, motioning toward a relatively clear spot inside near the Porsche. "Thanks," he continued, keeping his voice steady. "Just, you know, a few parts."

Bee's eyes gleamed like distant galaxies as she caught sight of Nick's car. "Wow, is that a Porsh?" she asked, her voice rich with admiration.

"Yes, it is," Nick replied. "Indeed," he added, feeling a surge of pride. "A classic. Took delivery last night." He made a small cheering forward motion with a strong arm and fist. But then his eyes flickered anxiously, scanning the surroundings for signs of intrusion, perpetually vigilant to safeguard his car and true identity.

Then she approached the Porsche, her eyes scanning it with delicate reverence as she set the packages down. "It's beautiful. I've always loved Porsh. There's just something about them," she mused.

"It's actually pronounced Por-sha," Nick clarified, his perfectionism surfacing. "And I'm getting a paint correction done on it." He tried to mitigate in advance any critical thoughts she might have about the icon. Whenever he spoke about cars, his apprehensions faded like fleets of paper sailboats quietly vanishing downstream.

"Oh, well, anyway, I haven't seen anyone here in a very long time. I've kept stacking up your packages. Did you just buy the place?" Her enthusiasm was infectious, although the garage was crumbling.

"Um, yes... yes, yes! I bought the place." Nick followed her lead. "I was just waiting for my car in order to move in. No use moving in without a car to work on." Nick played along, then forced a chuckle.

"Nice! Well, congrats!" she exclaimed. "You sure have a lot of deliveries to open." She looked behind him at a pile.

"It's a beauty, even with the swirl marks," Nick reverted the conversation to the car, finishing with a smile, allowing warmth to seep through his guarded exterior. "It's a Porsche 911, uh, GT2, 3.6-liter, flat-six, M96.70, twin-turbocharged. I've got my work cut out for me, though," he rattled off, standing with pride.

"Oh, wow, well, that sounds, um, coool." A hair of suspicion and confusion came through, but she finished her words authentically.

"It's the 5th generation 911, also known as version 996 by Porsche, actually."

As they talked, Bee started grabbing additional packages from her vehicle. Nick found himself naturally wanting to help, and together, they unloaded his supplies, each moment punctuated with increased openness and even a bit of laughter. He'd forgotten how joyful and uplifting Earthlings were, and the anxiety of his secret life as an E.T. receded slightly under her friendly gaze.

He learned about Bee's life as a delivery driver—the music playing in her delivery truck, the peculiar characters she encountered along the way, her overtime pay for working on holidays, the desert sunset routes she enjoyed, her love for tennis, and her innate sense of adventure. She inquired about Nick's life, a fact that pleased him even as he remained elusive and fixated on the car.

"Classic cars are like treasures from another era," Bee said, lifting a package with a careful stance. "They remind me of simpler times when everything seemed more tactile and genuine, don't you think?" Her words resonated deeply. He understood those very sentiments.

"Absolutely," he responded, his voice softer. "They're pieces of history we can keep alive. This one here could be the best car in the universe, but we'll never know until we give it a little love. It's the *potential* in things."

Bee paused, setting down the packages. "And the potential in people," she added, *her* tone softer now. "Thanks for letting me see the Porsche and for chatting with me. This has been the highlight of my day." She looked up at him with sincerity and brushed a creamy stray lock of honey-blonde hair behind her ear, then gracefully tucked it into her hat.

"Thank you," Nick replied, offering a genuine white smile. "It's nice to have some company for a change." He then pointed to a small circular red tattoo on the inside crease of her arm the size of a dime. "Say, is that the Flower of Life?"

"Oh, yes. It's a symbol deeply embedded in many cultures and traditions across the ancient globe. A significant presence throughout ancient societies, actually."

"Yeah," he gently continued. "And maybe throughout the universe, too." As his tone became quiet, Bee slowed down to absorb his words.

"Yeah, I sometimes wonder what's out there," she whispered, gazing up at the brilliant blue sky and the mysterious white moon suspended in daytime glow.

They exchanged warm smiles, and for a moment, the cluttered, dusty garage became a vibrant place. The contest back on Vetu had vanished entirely. Nick's feelings about the race with its attached worries seemed to pause as he interacted with her, somehow slowing time.

"Well, I should get going," Bee finally said somewhat reluctantly, dusting off her brown, flat-front shorts. "But I'll see you around."

"Yeah, see you," Nick replied, trying to mask his disappointment. Bee climbed back into her vehicle, giving him one last bright smile and wave before driving off, leaving a swirl of dust down the trail.

Watching her go, Nick sighed, relieved yet somewhat regretful. As the sound of her truck faded, he stood in the garage doorway, the feeling of her presence and her honeysuckle scent lingering in the air. Despite his advanced engineering capabilities, his mission, and his alien origins, he found himself briefly connected to a human experience.

For a moment, he began reminiscing about the many times he'd met various people through his interest in propulsion systems but suddenly recalled how he'd missed his coffee in all of the early morning action. *What are cars without coffee?* he thought, humoring himself. He brewed a morning French press and began to ease back into focus.

Nick carefully ran a new yellow microfiber cloth over the Porsche's seat. The distinct aroma of aged leather mingled with the unique scent of the garage, while the sailing smell of coffee randomly wafted through the air at moments. His fingers traced the immaculate stitching from years ago, again pulling him into a rush of vivid memories. The gleaming cars, the roaring engines, the devout spectators—and the memories from Earth's moons past. He pondered how the world of automotive excellence had called him back with the seductive whispers of universal friends and fierce rivals.

Images of the races at Le Mans returned to his mind; he could almost hear the symphony of the tuned engines. He remembered the cool air in the early hours, the array of clouds playing hide and seek with the sun, and the crystal energy of the crowd, a thousand heartbeats echoing in the physical throbs of speedsters revving.

He spent hours captivated by the Porsche, lost in thought, in his human form, while perched on a rolling office chair that had seen better days.

The Porsche's allure held him in rapture as he envisioned possibilities. Its legendary design—The 911—a distinctive and timeless aesthetic, a graceful evolution without the loss of its original essence. The elegantly curved lines and signature sloping roof formed the iconic silhouette instantly identifiable. He rolled back in his chair and stared at its nose, which showcased the iconic golden Porsche crest elegantly framed by the notorious 996 teardrop headlights.

Nick began organizing wrenches and ratchets on a long, scarred wooden workbench. The stale air in the dilapidated garage carried the faint scent of metal and oil, grounding him once more.

When he later prepared for a quiet afternoon nap, the zing of a dirt bike filtered through the stillness, bringing his revving engine thoughts back to life. Nick peered through the scuffed broken windows beside the main door, catching sight of a young man streaking up the drive, a cloud of dust following him.

The teenage rider, with russet brown hair and a backward baseball cap, halted in front of the garage with a camouflage backpack. His hoodie was appropriate for the cool weather, yet he wore shorts. He dismounted his bright orange bike, popping his vape pen into his mouth. Nick stepped back from the window as the boy approached through the open front door. Curiosity practically radiated from him as he took in the sight of the garage and then immediately the gleaming black Porsche.

"Hey," the boy called, removing his cap and revealing a mop of messy hair. His flawless blue eyes darted around, taking in every detail while he puffed his vape pen. "What are you doing here?" His loaded backpack was bursting at a few seams, an extension of the emotions hidden behind his eyes. He had a large scab on the inside of his right ankle, undoubtedly a healing burn from the exhaust pipe of his bike.

Nick's guard came up. "I just moved in. I'm restoring a car," he said with a snooty tone, eyeing the vapor steam pluming through the air. "No smoking in the garage, kid," he demanded. "How old are you?" He waved his human hand under his nose to waft the vapor away.

The boy raised an eyebrow but complied, tucking the vape pen into his back pocket. "Sure thing. Name's Tyler, what's yours?" He squared up.

"I'm Nick, and where's your helmet? How old are you?"

"Seventeen," Tyler answered, crossing his arms and nodding at the black Porsche. "Been messing around with engines since I was a kid. Never seen a Porsh up close, though. Is that one in pretty good condition?"

"Well, it's important for me to focus right now!" Nick exclaimed, gesturing to the garage around him. "I've got a lot of work ahead." He tried to cut the conversation.

"So, you just invaded the place?" Tyler expressed his frustration. He took a quick puff of his vape pen, then swiftly returned it to his pocket.

Nick cringed at the word "invaded." His cultural background from Vetu had created a heightened sensitivity to that term. Additionally, he didn't want anyone to know that he had actually invaded Earth; the kid was right. He stepped up, wiping his hands on a rag. "It's not like that," Nick said tersely. "And I would appreciate it if there were no smoking in here!" he snapped.

"No smoking in here? First of all, it's vaping, not smoking. It's steam, not smoke!" Tyler raised his voice. "My rule is no living in here! How about that? Or just being in here!" Nick looked up in surprise. "This place belonged to my father. He passed away. My mom owns this place now. So, yeah, you've invaded the place!"

"Hey, listen, kid, I—I'm not an invader—I'm—"

Tyler interrupted him. "Invader, invader, invader! I'm calling the police!"

"Stop it!" Nick thundered.

Chapter Two

"Just let me stay, kid. I'm from outta town. I... I... I thought the place was abandoned. I'm just going to fix my car then go, okay, kid? Please don't tell anybody," Nick pleaded with the boy.

Tyler shrugged, more interested in the contents of the garage. His demeanor transitioned to indifference, likely how he regarded most things in his teenage life; however, a fondness for the car showed in his eyes as they darted about, resting appreciatively on the Porsche 996. His tone softened, "So, cool car. How'd you get your hands on that?"

Nick tensed, his defensive instincts kicking in. "I bought it from an auction, ehe, nothing special."

"Come on, it's a Porsh 911. It's special," Tyler insisted, stepping closer to the car. He touched the black paint and peered inside. Still contemplating his decision. "Planning any mods?"

Nick swallowed, feeling cornered. "Just some routine work. Nothing major. It's the first water-cooled Porsche," he opened up. "Complete redesign, actually, by a guy from Hong Kong, goes by the name Pinky."

"Pinky?" Tyler questioned the colorful name.

"Pinky Lai, actually. He probably saved Porsche from bankruptcy altogether."

Tyler's curiosity only grew but shifted back to the car. "Like, what routine work? Exhaust? Air intake?"

Nick deflected, feeling the weight of Tyler's probing questions. "Just some upgrades. It's old and needs some care. And it's pronounced Por-sha." His voice sprang with a perturbed inflection.

Tyler straightened, a hint of impatience in his eyes. "Look, I get it. You're secretive. But this garage is technically mine. It belonged to my dad. I'll be turning eighteen soon and taking full possession."

Nick's jaw clenched. "Ehe, stop saying I've invaded, though, ehe, that's not what's happening here."

Tyler met his gaze and analyzed Nick's body language and demeanor well. "Then explain it to me. Why do you seem so secretive about everything?" He continued to square up.

The palm branches beyond the garage windows cast shadows as twilight fell. They stretched like fingers onto the cold, cracked floor. Nick felt his isolation from Vetu acutely. The pressure to maintain secrecy while longing for acceptance pressed down on him. He knew his journey on Earth was fraught with risks, and revealing too much could jeopardize everything. He worried about his conspicuous spaceship parked out back, even though the tarp covered it.

Nick's tone remained at ease, though his words were still guarded. "It's complicated. But I'm not here to cause trouble. This car—this project—means something very important to me... To my heart, kid."

Tyler's face tightened with a mix of determination and defiance. "This garage means something to me, too. And if we can't find a way to share it, then that's going to be a problem. I should set some rules. I honestly don't think you should be here, actually. How long are you staying?" Tyler gathered his thoughts aloud.

Nick thought he would be kicked out immediately, yet he could see the allure of the sleek Porsche held Tyler's interest. Excitement was probably rare in the quiet desolation of the tiny ghost town.

Nick nodded reluctantly in disbelief that things on Earth were already getting out of hand. "Fine," he conceded. "The first rule is no vaping around me." He held firm, setting his own rule first. He wasn't going down without a fight. He'd traveled a lengthy distance and put far too much into the project to back down.

Tyler exhaled sharply through his nose, then swiftly stole a whisper from his vape pen, returning it to his pocket with a sleight of hand. "Deal. But I want in. I want to help with the car. My dad taught me a lot about mechanics, and I can be useful." He paused. "You don't have to pay me. I just want to learn and drive the car... once in a while." His words trailed off, and he refocused on the 996.

Nick hesitated, feeling the weight of his past blending with the present. The boy, standing firm in his rightful place,

21

reminded him of his ambitions back on Vetu and the complex dance of craftsmanship and legacy. However, he could sense Tyler's deep connection to the garage, more profound than his own bond with the Porsche and the race.

Tyler was a handsome boy in all ways. He could have been out with his friends or spending time doing anything else. Nick's thoughts meandered. This seventeen-year-old, who had now unwittingly become entangled in his quest, mirrored his own curiosity and once youthful exuberance, stirring memories of his early days in the automotive world before the WCACCV2 named him Old Dog. The boy's eagerness to learn was a dash of hope, yet it brought forth a pang of anxiety.

"Alright," Nick finally agreed, his voice a mix of wariness and desire. "We can figure something out, but no more calling me invader!"

Tyler extended his hand, the glint of determination in his eyes. "Agreed. And maybe, you'll trust me enough to share what's really going on here."

Nick shook his head in disbelief and then shook Tyler's hand, but the garage began to wane as a prison of secrets and feel more like a place where, perhaps, trust could be built. After all, he thought, the kid was lonely and wasn't trying to hurt anyone.

Nick's thoughts drifted back to the exhilarating Le Mans, unleashing a flood of vivid memories once again. He saw himself seated among a sea of spectators, the air buzzing with excitement. There was something intoxicating about the camaraderie shared among car enthusiasts. It was a connection that transcended language and culture, worlds and galaxies, binding them through a shared love for speed and engineering marvels. He remembered the fervent conversations with strangers, united by their admiration for the sleek machines slinging around the track. Those moments had ignited a spark within him, a passion that propelled him not just on Earth but onto this very quest. Perhaps Tyler was just another person growing into the same shared passions.

His attention turned to the smeared, shattered garage window as Tyler departed down the dirt drive, and the treble-fluting pitch of his vibrant orange dirt bike reverberated through the jagged cracks of the windows.

Nick's thoughts meandered back to the stern rules of the WCACCV2. He wiped the sweat from his brow as the rhythmic clinking of tools echoed through the garage while he organized his workbench. He considered mutating into his more agile E.T. form for better movement; however, he hesitated, unsure of how many unexpected guests he would need to accommodate that afternoon, as transforming required a significant drain on his life force.

It wasn't long before Tyler returned on his zinging dirt bike. In fact, it was the very next afternoon.

"Hey, Nick," Tyler called out, his voice echoed through the cavernous garage. "I know we didn't get off to the best start yesterday, but you're right. The garage *is* just sitting here, and I really want to help you with that Porsche. I know my way around dirt bikes and mechanical repairs, and I think I can help."

Nick paused, scrutinizing Tyler's earnest expression. He'd pondered the potential risks—revealing too much, getting too close. Yet the possibility of forging a tentative alliance nudged at the back of his mind. Moreover, it *was* Tyler's garage, and they had already shaken hands on it; on Earth, that meant a lot to some people—a world where their word was their bond. *Especially in America,* Nick thought.

Perhaps having an extra pair of hands wouldn't be such a bad idea. His gaze shifted to the Porsche, resting under the soft beams of mosaic hues. The web of light rays danced across the cracked floor, fragmented from the broken and spidered glass, through the dirty windows.

His gaze then followed the curtain of colors to the old, peeling wooden panes surrounding them, his hand raised to his chin as he thought. He thought of how the afternoon sun was the brightest part of the day inside the old garage. Then he thought of being in his brown study back home, a place where he researched, read books and contemplated.

Tyler watched for a moment, his expression steady with a mixture of curiosity and determination as he inched closer to Nick, who maintained stoicism. He sat on a small wooden crate, straddling it, waiting patiently. Then he tilted his chin up to direct a soft vibration of words toward Nick's direction. "I can clean the windows, too," Tyler hinted.

"No!" Nick slightly snapped, springing his shoulders and rotating to face the boy. Tyler slouched back, losing his gain.

"I don't want people to see in here. You know..." he lightly continued. "It's not just any car," Nick said, his tone guarded. "It's a racer! Okay?" He raised his volume again and tried emphatically opening up to Tyler.

"I get it," Tyler responded, his voice eager yet respectful, but he didn't understand. He continued speaking, "My dad used to work on cars, too. The garage was our place. It's where I learned everything I know. Being here feels right. I want to contribute, as we agreed."

"This project isn't something I take lightly," Nick added. He noticed the nostalgic glimmer in Tyler's eyes, a kindred spirit recalling fond times with his dad. Possibly, this was a way for Tyler to keep the memories of his father alive. He felt a pang of resonance. He, too, had memories of learning the intricacies of mechanics, guided by the hands of a mentor. The words hung between them, the air thick with shared yet unspoken bonds of loss and passion.

"Alright," Nick said finally, his voice softening. "You can help with some minor tasks, but you have to wait awhile and just watch, let me figure out a job for you, and no vaping around here. Those fumes, they—just keep it away!"

"Deal!" Tyler grinned, holding up his vape pen without puffing and then sliding it into the back pocket of his jeans.

The boy confidently showcased the organizational skills he had developed, maybe while tidying the shop for his father. After all, it was his own right to clean his dad's garage. The moist scent of engine oil and sweat now clung to him as well, a familiar comfort in the desert breeze that barely flowed through the stale garage.

As Tyler began assisting with small tasks, like removing the taillights from the 996 to buff them, Nick taught him,

"There is a ten-millimeter hex socket needed on each rear light. It's simple, but go ahead and pop the deck lid first."

Nick pointed at the deck lid release button by the driver-side door sill and watched with a scrutinizing eye. He saw potential in Tyler. His young, strong, and steady hands were precise. The rhythmic clacks of the ratchet filled the space as Tyler began to follow Nick's directions.

"Those are M6 bolts. That means they are six millimeters in diameter, and they have a thread pitch of one millimeter. Don't strip'em, or we won't get'em back in. Well, I could... but it would take all day." Nick expressed the depth of his knowledge aloud, so Tyler could come to terms with whom he was working alongside.

After a moment of rest, Tyler ventured outside, and worry set over Nick that the hidden spacecraft might be discovered in the back drive. But Tyler soon returned through the front door, beaming with pride as he clutched a coconut. "Thirsty?" he asked, lifting it as if to make a toast. Uncertain, Nick simply watched Tyler in silence.

Tyler approached the workbench to drill the coconut. Then he struck the end with a hammer and chisel, punching a clear hole in it. He raised the coconut in triumph, took a swig, and then moved closer to Nick, offering it to him.

"The three palm trees outside are coconut palms. My dad planted them after a trip to Florida with my mom... before they divorced," he concluded, his voice tinged with sadness. Mimicking Tyler, Nick took a compassionate swig from the coconut.

"Yeah, it tastes great."

"We've got three trees. They're the only coconut palms I know of in the desert. Just be careful. If one falls on your head, it'll crack you open instead." He laughed.

"Ah, a twist of fate," Nick quickly understood.

"My dad called them the three wise men."

"Wise men?" Nick asked, intrigued.

"Yeah, like the three wise men who bared gifts."

"Oh, um, right, of course." Nick tried to hide his confused tone.

The day sailed away as the horizon glowed like molten gold sprinkled with violet sand. With each passing moment, Nick felt a shift. The crumbling walls of his secrecy began to crack as he felt a small connection to Tyler's respectful, hard-working, and optimistic nature. The boy's questions about torx bolts, German engineering, and suspension were met with Nick's guarded but gradually warming responses.

"I remember fixing up dirt bikes with my dad," Tyler shared again, his voice carrying a soft tremor. "We spent hours in the garage, just like this, talking about everything. Those were the best times."

Nick nodded, a silent acknowledgment of the sentiment. He thought again of Vetu and of his old mentor, who had instilled in him a love for mechanics, just as Tyler's father had. Memories of sleek hovercars and advanced propulsion systems flashed through his mind, presenting a vast contrast to the vintage charm of the 996 resting before them.

"You know," Nick began, choosing his words carefully, "Where I come from, car culture is a big deal, too. Maybe not exactly like here, but it connects people."

Tyler looked up, a newfound respect in his eyes. "Exactly. It's not just about the cars—that's what my dad said. By the way, where are you from? England or something? You sound British."

"Ha!" Nick objected. "We taught the British English, mate. Actually, I speak Galactic English. Originally stems from something like German, actually."

"Galactic English? What does that mean?"

Nick backpedaled, "Yeah, it's just a British style, mate. Closer to... um... Ireland." His struggle for concealment continued.

As the sun released the last of its evening colors and the darkness softly stroked the cool evening air, the pair worked in companionable silence, punctuated by snippets of new conversation. The boy continued to organize the garage while Nick made his list of parts. Tyler's gentle prodding and genuine curiosity gradually drew out more details from Nick—details about the modifications he'd planned, his ambitions, and, ultimately, how Nick wasn't merely restoring the car; he was transforming it into a high-performance racer, ready for the track and spotlight. However, he avoided answering Tyler's question regarding the race's whereabouts, casually mentioning that he would disclose the details later.

Tyler's eyes widened with each revelation as he absorbed the information with an eager mind. "So, you're telling me this car might actually win a race?"

Nick allowed himself a small, rare smile. "It has to! That is if we do things right."

"How many races have you been in?" Tyler asked.

"Over twelve hundred, mate."

"Wow!" Tyler exclaimed. "How many have you won?"

"Well, over half."

"Woah," Tyler added, slowly turning quiet.

Nick continued. "You see, my friends call me Old Dog. I can't stand it anymore. They used to have respect for me when I won races. I just don't win anymore."

"Why don't you win?"

"Well… I don't know. I don't really know why," he answered, mystified himself.

Tyler didn't pry. They just worked alongside each other, the camaraderie growing with each shared tool, and exchanged glance. While they worked, Nick opened the car's front trunk compartment and explained that many people mistakenly referred to it as a 'frunk' due to its positioning since the engine is located in the rear of the car and there is no trunk. He clarified the term as inaccurate, the correct designation being 'front storage.' He then retrieved the Porsche's factory emergency toolkit from the front storage to show Tyler how the headlights were released with Porsche's OEM 5-millimeter hex headlight removal tool.

Nick went on to explain that OEM stood for Original Equipment Manufacturer. However, he soon found himself quietly exhausted by the relentless energy demanded to engage with Tyler, especially while maintaining his human guise. It was testing to embrace the life of a mechanic when he was operating in a body that wasn't his own. Each time Nick imparted a lesson, Tyler's curiosity only deepened, his questions spiraling into an infinite labyrinth. At times, Nick wished the boy would leave so he could rest in his own green skin.

But in the dusty, dim garage, amidst the clinks and the soft blow of the cool desert winter wind, a bond was being forged—one that promised to endure, like the machines they both cherished.

That evening, Tyler's mother rang his mobile, calling him home for dinner. With his remaining determination, he revved the engine of his dirt bike again and zipped down the road. As Nick watched him fade away, an echo of his own childhood surfaced—a longing for old times he sometimes wished to relive. An opportunity to create a family of his own had yet to knock on his door. He occasionally weighed whether his aspirations would transform into reality or fade into mere illusions as time passed.

The following morning after sunrise, Nick stood in the soft morning light of the quiet garage with a hot cup of coffee, alone again in his rubbery, comfortable skin. He organized the backlog of deliveries, breaking down each box and setting things for the day.

Metallic tangs trapped in the garage and whiffs of oil permeated the air as he cleared his nostrils and palate with the steam and slurps of his hot coffee. He began on the Porsche, masking the complex emotions that swirled within him. Each tool he began to use weighed down by burdens of secrecy. He felt the sting of isolation, a second shadow cast by his alien nature. Concealing his identity truly took a toll, though it seemed necessary to protect both himself and those he interacted with on Earth.

Tyler's presence in the garage was both a comfort and a trial. The young man's energy was infectious, though marred by the effort required for Nick to maintain his human appearance.

He continued to put one foot in front of the other and eventually finalized the list of parts needed for the next phase—each item critical for breathing new life into the 996. He dialed the distant Porsche dealership, located an hour into the city, and pressed 'one' for the parts department.

"Good afternoon, Porsche of Las Vegas, this is Kiev Eichman. How can I help you today?" The voice on the other end was clear and professional, reminding Nick of the immaculate Porsche museum in Stuttgart, Germany he'd visited many moons ago.

Taking a deep breath, Nick steadied himself. "Hi, this is Nick Bates. I need to order a new front hood—the bonnet lid, for a 996, two additional bonnet shocks, and a replacement shock for the rear deck lid. I'm in the middle of a restoration project."

"Certainly, Mr. Bates." Kiev's voice was calm and reassuring, a contrast to Nick's chaos percolating. "Let me check our inventory for those parts. May I place you on a brief hold?"

"Okay."

As the line went quiet, Nick paused his pacing. His eyes wandered over the natural light rising in the garage, then to the artificial burning filaments strung through the tall ceiling.

Many tools still lay scattered, but the remnants of past repairs were now stacked in the cluttered corners of the garage. He could hear the faint hum of his ETV, which honed power through the makeshift electric vehicle charger he'd rigged. Each sound and visual detail anchored him in the moment, grounding his mind in the task at hand.

"Mr. Bates? We do have the shocks in stock, and the bonnet lid will be available within two days," Kiev relayed, with a touch of satisfaction in his tone. "Is there anything else I can assist you with?" As the conversation continued, Nick requested a few more parts and trim clips. "Would you like me to go ahead and place an order for those items?"

"Uh, yeah, that would be great. Yeah, please do," Nick replied, unable to dampen the eagerness from his voice. The idea of maintaining a steady pace was pulling him through the fog of uncertainty that had arisen from the weight of the daily distractions he now faced.

Nick's confidence grew, and the nervous energy that had gripped him slowly settled. He confirmed his order with meticulous detail, ensuring accuracy in each step of his quest for perfection. This was more than just a restoration project; it was the only bridge connecting him from his recent, dull past to a bright, fresh future.

"Thank you, Mr. Bates. Your order is all set and will be ready soon. Is there anything else I can assist you with today?" Kiev's efficiency and knowledge of Porsche brought a sense of camaraderie, easing the solitude that Nick often felt.

"I may need to book a service appointment. There's some horrible rattling under the car. I think there are multiple things wrong under there. Who would I talk to about that?"

"Well, I can help you. I'm actually the classic car service advisor," he announced.

"Oh, really? Well, that's nice."

"Yes, any Porsche put in service over twenty years ago," he confirmed.

"Well, I'll call you back. There are a few things I need to check on. Maybe when I come down to get the parts, I'll drop it off for a complete inspection."

"Sure, just let me know ahead of time so I can schedule you. We get pretty busy back there."

"Thank you, Kiev. I appreciate your help, mate," Nick said, a genuine smile forming. He ended the call and silently slipped his mobile phone back into his pocket.

Standing amidst the scattered tools, morning glow, and the early, timid, ghostly shadows, Nick felt a wave of empowerment wash over him. Each ordered part was a step closer to reclaiming a joyful piece of his reputation on Vetu.

With renewed determination, Nick propped back his shoulders, imagining the brilliance of freshly installed upgrades and overhauls. He let his gaze travel across the dimly lit space filled with the promise of renewal. He could see the completed project in his mind's eye, envisioning the hanging bulbs reflecting the majesty of its restored surface and listening to the symphony of its engine.

He imagined rolling up the bay doors, coming out of his isolation, burning rubber on the highways, and the landscape of Earth flashing by. For a brief moment, he envisioned Bee in his mind, her laughter mingling with the hum of the engine, her presence an unexpected but welcome addition to his solitary pursuits.

He took a deep breath and mentally mapped out other tasks. A blend of mechanical thoughts and personal stakes fueled a relentless passion.

He stepped back and turned for a moment. "Something has to be done about these darn human headlights," he spoke aloud to himself, snapping back into focus. He gazed at the chipped workbench now housing the old, foggy lenses.

The road ahead was clear. Each step, every part, brought him closer not only to a completed racer but to the realization of dreams entwined across galaxies and time.

Chapter Three

The boy had been coming and going from the garage briefly after school, slowly putting pressure on Nick as he concealed his true identity. But Nick hadn't seen the boy for a few days and was deeply immersed in his new surroundings, establishing his routines.

The dim rays of the abandoned garage lit the thick, dusty air as it clung to Nick's green skin, but his true alien form showed no hint of discomfort. He examined the Porsche headlights, their once-pristine glow now tainted by a web of micro-scratches, swirl marks, and oxidized haze.

With warmth, he recalled days at home, cruising down those dusky roads when the crimson and amber fading suns opposed each other. The breeze always flowed gracefully across his shiny, domed forehead while his various speedsters had illuminated the twilight with the glow of their laser headlamps. It was time to revive that brilliance here with the infamous 996.2 teardrop headlights.

First, he gathered warm, soapy water and, with reverence, tenderly cleaned the outer lenses. As he rinsed away the grime, a wave of fondness washed over him, reminiscent of lazy afternoons when every detail mattered.

Once the old lights were squeaky clean, the first phase began. With his tacky, lobed fingers, Nick pinched his array of sandpapers. Each grit had its purpose; higher numbers indicated smoother finishes, so he grabbed the coarse sandpaper first.

The initial step of his secret restoration recipe involved gently dry sanding with 600-grit paper. With the electric tool set to the lowest setting, he meticulously sanded in straight horizontal strokes, ensuring every inch of the surface received attention. He was relentless in his pursuit, feeling a tinge of nostalgia with each pass as if he were channeling memories of the countless projects he'd undertaken. He watched for any particularly stubborn oxidized areas where he might need to use the 400-grit paper for a brief moment, but he never ran into trouble.

As he paused the electric tool, he suddenly heard the sound of Tyler's hot motorbike approaching the garage; it was much too near—the wheels now crunching over the gravel. Tyler had already arrived. The noise of Nick's electric sander had muffled the sound of the zinging bike, which Nick could usually hear clearly as it approached down the long, private drive.

Quickly, as Tyler twisted the doorknob to the shop, Nick, still in his green birthday suit, inhaled deeply and executed his invisible illusion.

"Hey, Mr. Bates! How's the Porsh coming along... Porsha?" The boy called out. His eyes darted over the car and the array of tools. Nick dashed beside him, completely unseen, up the plank wooden stairs to his loft and concealed himself in the back corner, far behind the overlooking rail. Then he released his breath as he simultaneously shifted into human form and slipped into jeans and a T-shirt.

"Hey, Tee, I'll be down in a minute!" Nick's voice echoed to the shop below as he assigned Tyler a nickname. It couldn't hurt. He needed to be in Tyler's good graces if he ever found himself exposed as an extraterrestrial. As adrenaline surged through him, he descended the stairs and greeted Tyler, irritation seeping through his exhaustion. "It's coming. Shouldn't you be in school?" His dismissive undertone was a cold shoulder.

"School's over for today," Tyler replied as he gazed around at the garage and noticed how Nick had begun nesting. He set his graphic helmet on the black seat of the dirt bike. "I wanted to see your progress." He maintained a good attitude. Tyler was tough, buoyant, and resilient.

"Okay, okay, please just watch because I'm right in the middle of a project," he said while returning to the workbench.

Tyler nodded. "Weren't you just changing, though?" His brow furrowed in suspicion.

"Eha, I was doing both! At the same time!" Nick snarked.

"Where are your shoes?" Tyler looked down at Nick's bare feet.

"Let's talk later! Just work now!" he said, springing his head.

Nick resumed the project, attempting to return to his meditative state before Tyler interrupted. He concentrated on performing the smooth motions, which were more difficult now in human form.

Nonetheless, the next phase was wet sanding, armed with 1,000-grit sandpaper. Nick spritzed the surface with water to serve as a lubricant and began with gentle sanding. His motions were consistent, his emotions, not so much. He embraced the hum and rhythm of the tool, finding his solace in the task once again.

Tyler maintained a watchful presence from a comfortable distance, gradually easing Nick's tension. Nick continually replenished the water, allowing his tool to glide effortlessly across the lens, making the task not only effective but also soothing.

With each step, he restored not just the headlights but a glimmer in his heart, intertwining memories with the promise of adventures yet to come.

At this stage, the headlights were noticeably clear, but Nick soon switched to 2,000-grit sandpaper to achieve a pristine appearance. He treated the surface with care, applying water once more as he continued the sanding ritual, repeating the process. In those moments, surrounded by the now-comfortable sights of his workshop, he felt a deep connection to his car and the joy it brought him.

Next, with the cloudy layer gone, the lights were much more transparent and almost looked new. However, Nick wanted that showroom sparkle, so he began to clean and polish the lenses. First, he wiped the surfaces with alcohol and fresh yellow towels, removing all the sanding debris. He reached for the acrylic and plastics polishing compound—a mild-cut clay bar, to produce the most exceptional finish tailored for the job.

As the unique cotton buffing wheel vibrated and whirled to life, memories of the dual suns dipping below the marigold horizon reclaimed his mind's eye. He sank into a zone. Steady from years of space engineering and mechanics, his hand ran the buffer across the headlights in deliberate, practiced motions as he finished buffing them out to perfection.

To properly complete the restoration, he applied three layers of UV sealant to the first headlight and instructed Tyler to mirror him with the second, ensuring the vibrant new shine remained intact and safeguarded against future oxidation.

When the task was complete, Nick screwed the cap back onto the bottle of polish and explained to Tyler, "You've gotta use the lowest setting with the power tools. Otherwise, you'll slowly melt the acrylic before you know it. And you'll kill the lights altogether."

"Kind of like slowly turning up the heat and boiling a frog to death?" Tyler rallied up a laugh.

"No!" Nick exclaimed, jumping. "No. Never!" he furrowed his brow and trampled off to the adjacent bathroom.

Once he regained his composure and acknowledged the reality, he returned to quietly clean up the workbench.

"What if I can't remember any of this?" Tyler broke the silence, attempting to ease the awkwardness that had suspiciously developed.

"Eha, well, I hope you don't," Nick snapped.

"No, really. I mean the buffing process. Some people can't even do this," he remarked.

Nick looked at Tyler. "Well, you know what you do then?" Tyler stared back at him. "You pay me to do it! Haha."

"How much?" Tyler pushed back the sarcasm.

"We're looking at a full overhaul," Nick changed the subject, ragging the mop over the water on the floor, dodging it with his bare feet. "New air intake, all custom modifications. It needs to perform like a racer to win."

Tyler's eyes lit up. "That's awesome! I bet this thing is going to roar once it's all said and done." He looked at the car. "What other mods are you thinking?"

"Lots, but let's just say it's going to have more than just looks," Nick replied, a hint of warmth creeping into his guarded voice. Despite himself, Nick couldn't help but feel a flicker of hope—that maybe this partnership could lead to something worthwhile. "How about you? What do you know about mods?"

"Well," Tyler said, pushing out his bottom lip for a moment, "Mostly dirt bikes. My dad was a genius with mechanics, kind of like you. He taught me plenty before he… you know."

Nick nodded, understanding the unspoken loss. Tyler's sincerity and shared memories drew Nick closer, urging him to open up, yet his fear loomed like a dark cloud.

Nick decided to lift the spirits in the room by playing some music through the Porsche's stereo system and booming subwoofer tucked behind its bucket seats. He attempted to sync his smartphone with what he called the "ol' Bluetooth" technology the Porsche hosted through its head unit. After his efforts were unsuccessful due to the advanced nature of his phone, he turned to Tyler for help.

"Hey, Tyler, will you connect your phone here and play some tunes? This thing's got a nice eight-inch audio subwoofer. We have those back home. Heavy, expensive son of a gun."

Tyler easily connected his phone by tapping several areas on the Porsche's head unit and its colorful seven-inch LED display. The young boy's swiftness and enthusiasm invigorated the shop's atmosphere.

With a curious expression, he pointed at Nick's transparent mobile device, which was resting on the driver's seat and resembled only the slender glass surface of his own phone. "Is that your phone? I've never seen anything like that! Where did you get it?" he questioned with an urgent and passionate curiosity. He kept his hands to himself, but his eyes fixated on the crystal device.

Nick's pulse quickened as he grasped the phone and slipped it into his pocket, turning to face Tyler with a guarded look. "Rare model," he said curtly. "Eha, not important right now! Play some Motown."

Tyler's intrigue remained undeterred. "I was thinking if you can get those around here—"

"Later!" Nick cut in, his eyes narrowing. "I need music to focus!"

In Nick's mind, echoes of social gatherings on Vetu collided with the sound of Tyler's eager inquiries, spiking his fear of discovery, stirring an internal battle between connection and isolation. He knew Tyler meant well, but each moment of engagement threatened the delicate state of the secret mission.

Suddenly, the Porsche made a strange electronic noise, and the dashboard lights flickered in unison with the music, startling both of them and snapping their attention to the car, puzzled.

Tyler looked as though he had seen a ghost. His gaze then shifted suspiciously toward the partially open back door, where the blue tarp covering the spacecraft flapped violently in the fierce desert gusts.

Nick glanced at the Porsche's dashboard, searching for the key at the ignition left of the steering wheel. Quickly abandoning that pursuit, he swiftly strode back to his spacecraft to retrieve his scanner, ensuring the back door was fully closed behind him. "Be right back. Stay here!" his tone demanded urgently. He secured the blue solar tarp and retrieved the scanner.

Upon returning with the device, he adjusted it, his wide eyes narrowed as he scanned the interior, sweeping the wand around until an R.F. signal intensified near the glove compartment. "Bonsoir, Monsieur?" a female computer voice sounded.

He set the wand on the front passenger seat to free his hand, stretched across from the driver's side, and attempted to open the glove compartment, but the latch resisted. With a determined pull, he finally dislodged it, revealing a silver aluminum Acme AI unit—an aftermarket artificial intelligence package that shouldn't have been accessible on Earth for another seven decades. It had been forced to fit, stuffed inside, and placed extreme pressure on the compartment door.

He swiftly removed the slightly bulky device, feeling the cool satin aluminum beneath his touch. It bore a striking resemblance to a car stereo amplifier, with crafted finned heat sinks built into its design. From the glove compartment, he moved it to a clean area on the long workbench, noticing its dangling, smashed connector. "Incredible! A worthless Acme!" he exclaimed as he scanned the vicinity for Tyler, who had now disappeared.

Nick turned back to his work, but after a few minutes, he realized that Tyler was no longer in sight. Panic swelled within him as he called out, "Tyler? Where'd you go, Tee?"

A jolt of alarm shot through him when he didn't receive an immediate answer. Seconds later, he heard the unmistakable rustling of the tarp outside again. Bursting out of the back door, he found Tyler standing frozen, his eyes wide with astonishment, staring at the smooth alien spacecraft hidden beneath the blue, flapping cover.

"What the—what is this thing?" Tyler's voice wavered as fear tinged his expression. The reality of the spacecraft defied everything Earthlings knew.

"We'll talk! Oh, we'll talk!" Nick exclaimed, trying to decide how to explain.

Suddenly, Tyler attempted to bolt, to flee around the house, but Nick clenched his arm.

"I can explain, it's an ETV, but you need to keep it a secret!"

Tyler belted out, "Ahhhhhhh!"

On an impulse, Nick flashed from his human guise to his green alien skin, showing Tyler his authentic origins. "I'm an invader!" he hollered, trying to scare the boy. "Stop, or I'll melt your brain!" he continued with an angry bluff, as humans believed extraterrestrials could do anything. Then, he instantly mutated back to his human form to ease Tyler.

Tyler stopped struggling, a mix of confusion and more fear flooding his features as he took shallow breaths. "Melt my brain?" he stammered. Tyler was shocked and dazed.

"Like soup," Nick dampened his tone, then sighed, releasing his grip but still holding Tyler's gaze. "Yes, Tyler. I'm not from Earth. I'm an extraterrestrial from Planet Vetu." His words hung heavily, the truth finally unveiled. "But, listen, you can't tell anyone!"

"What?"

"I'll teach you everything about the Porsche!" Nick started, frantically selling himself. "We'll work as equal partners—hand in hand, right by each other's side, mate," he continued as Tyler still stared at him blankly in bewilderment. "I have three hundred years of experience!" he paused and waited for Tyler to say something, but nothing came out. The boy was frozen. "I can teach you how to become invisible, kid!" Nick put on a fake grin, worried as ever.

"I want to go home," Tyler uttered softly with his desperate face; the gleam in his eyes from earlier had vanished.

"Just hang out awhile. I'll take you for a drive in the Porsche and let *you* drive it. I'll teach you how to drive a stick shift, mate. I won't hurt you, I promise. Please stay awhile."

Nick's tone turned soft, authentic, and urgent for acceptance, and Tyler began to understand.

"Why are you here?" he questioned Nick.

"Well, for social standing, mate, back home, they call me Old Dog! You see, there's a race, and I used to be a racer. Well, I *am* a racer! I just don't *win* anymore! I hate that they call me Old Dog."

"Is your name really Nick?"

"Absolutely, kid, that's my real name, Nick R. Bates. I've got a mere six months to transform this GT2 into a proper racer and transport it back to my galaxy in my spaceship to clinch the victory. The following day, there's a car show, too. There's a comprehensive set of regulations posted on that board inside." He gestured back to the shop, hoping to sell Tyler on his intentions. "I'm telling the truth." Nick rested his hand on Tyler's shoulder, gently steering him back toward the garage. "We can check out the spaceship later." Tyler nodded in agreement as they stepped over the cords of the spliced electric vehicle chargers connected to the transfer switch. The boy followed the wires with his eyes, noticing the cords tracked back to the aluminum spaceship under the tarp.

Nick wasn't sure if Tyler would suddenly try to flee again, but he could see that the promise of hidden knowledge intrigued the boy. He thought his fear could slowly transition into fascination. "Seriously? You can teach me all of that?" His skepticism lingered, but it was overshadowed by his curiosity.

"Yes," Nick affirmed, his voice softer now, carrying an edge of vulnerability. "But only if you keep all this quiet. Understand?"

"Alright," Tyler whispered, nodding slowly as the weight of the revelation seemed to settle over him. "What does ETV mean, anyway?"

Nick felt a glimmer of hope. "Good. Now, let's get back to work. There's a lot you need to learn. And it means Extraterrestrial Vehicle," he answered.

Nick's wariness slightly diminished by Tyler's confirmation. "I have three hundred years of experience," Nick restated, offering a small, hesitant smile. "You'll learn from the best."

"You're three hundred years old?"

"Technically, yes, in human years. Our solar planet revolves around the suns very differently. You know, science and stuff. They've been calling me Old Dog for fifty years."

"Wow," Tyler said, still in awe, gazing at the Porsche.

"Well, let's shake all this off and go for a ride, yeah?"

"Okay, what's the difference between the 911, 996, GT2, and a Carrera?" Tyler asked, apparently feeling at ease to express himself more freely now that the dynamic between them had shifted.

"Great question!" Nick responded encouragingly. "I'll tell you about it while we investigate this Acme AI system I found in the glovebox when the radio went berserk." Nick led him over to the workbench, where the Acme box was lying next to the drying headlamps. As he attempted to disassemble it for inspection, he fumbled the screwdriver awkwardly with his human hand, longing to revert to his alien form.

Chapter Four

Nick concentrated intently on the task at hand. Beneath the faint glow of the coned bench light, he scrutinized the Acme hardware, discovering multiple frayed wires. With expert knowledge but muddling through with human fingers, he carefully reconnected each wire within the module, utilizing soldering tools and surgical binocular loupes. His unfaltering, intricate dance of metal and silicon would bring the Acme AI back to life. Yet, in the rust and shadows of the earthly garage, it seemed out of place. The technology was a relic to him but too sophisticated for the current surroundings.

Nick carefully trimmed the heat sink fins on the aluminum case with tin snips and the mounted yellow table grinder. He planned to seamlessly fit the hardware back into the glovebox, using care to avoid any re-pinching of the wires.

Once the repairs and trim were complete, he continued to custom-fit an on-off toggle switch to the device so that, if it malfunctioned at any point, he could quickly power it off. Finally, he stretched upright, wiping his hands on a grease-stained rag, and headed to reinstall the Acme unit. Carefully, he slid into the passenger seat of the Porsche 996 while Tee settled into the driver's side and observed intently, captivated by the unfolding scene.

The quality leather creaked under their weight, the shadows deepening as the amber dashboard illuminated, now alive with the reactivated Acme AI. As long as it was connected to the car, the absence of a key didn't phase the unit; the Acme system was fully capable of autonomous operation.

The car suddenly bleeped and spoke, startling them. "Bonsoir, Monsieur?" the female computer voice reset.

Feeling startled by the voice and knowing the history of the box, Nick shouted in frustration, "I don't understand French!"

"Good evening, sir," it responded, seamlessly switching to the local English.

Nick let out a sigh in the quiet expanse of the garage, the grease towel still in his hand. Previous car meets he had attended flashed before his eyes, recalling the era when Acme AI thrived on his planet. The units were built into all new vehicles, and the Acme Company supplied aftermarket units for existing models. But he remembered how the systems ultimately faded into obscurity, how they were seen as unimportant because they couldn't provide useful information about propulsion system vitals. The units had become dull companions.

There were a few fanatics who began the Acme AI saga and continued in a cultish manner, the ones who fell in love, but they were few.

He also remembered his barbarous competitor, Karl Cruze, the pale, gray-skinned founder and original engineer behind Acme AI. Karl had unscrupulously exploited the technology to record conversations within the vehicles of unsuspecting buyers. This unethical practice continued until various governments in Vetu enacted privacy legislation against it, leading to the dismantling and sale of Karl's network as fragmented assets.

"Karl," he muttered under his breath. The name brought a bitter taste to his mouth. Karl's assortment of stained and tattered scarves, scorched by burn marks from his fat cigars, reflected a profound disregard for self. While Karl was synonymous with high-end tech and supreme engineering skills, Nick associated him with treachery and underhanded tactics. He was physically out of shape, but that wasn't all. His emotionally bent-out-of-shape and distraught personality often drove people away. This AI device represented a specter of past conflicts and rivalries that Nick longed to leave behind. Although, he knew he had to face Karl back home in the galactic race ahead.

Not overly eager to discover its old capabilities, Nick put the AI software to the test, confronting it with a series of questions to determine its functionality and see if it could offer any useful advice about the Porsche.

"What's your name?" he asked.

"What do you want it to be, sir?" it responded.

"Snuffleupagus," said Nick. Tee laughed out loud.

"Okay, how may I help you?"

"What year was the first, ehe, Porsche... 996 put into production?"

"The 5th generation 911 first debuted at the 1997 Frankfurt Motor Show, referred to internally as the 996 by Porsche AG. The Carrera Coupe variant was available for sale in Europe shortly thereafter," she said. "Would you like to know more?"

"Yes," Nick responded.

"Your GT2 is the high-performance, track-oriented version of the 911. The GT2 has a turbocharged engine that delivers significantly more horsepower than the other base 911 models, AKA Carrera models."

"List all of the 996 models for my friend Tee." He prompted.

"Carrera base model, Carrera S, Carrera 4—all-wheel drive, Carrera 4S, Turbo, Turbo S, GT3, GT3 RS, Targa, Cabriolet, GT2—,"

"Okay, stop!" Nick snapped. "It's all the same car. There are over ten variants of the 996 kid—they're all 911s!"

"Okay." Tee was monotone.

"What's the quote about a Porsche resembling a frog?" Nick continued.

"A Porsche will always look like a Porsche. My grandfather took these shapes from nature, so the headlamps of the 911 maybe look a little like the eyes of a frog, but it comes from nature, and the best shapes are from nature, so why change? - Ferdinand Alexander Porsche - German designer and grandson of Ferdinand Porsche."

"Wow!" Tee's excitement amplified.

Nick paused in the passenger seat, his left hand resting on the car's shifter. He let out a sigh and looked away against the remaining daylight morphing through the cracked windows. This AI wasn't just any piece of technology but a relic from his past, a symbol of disappointment and mistrust.

His mind replayed more scenes from Vetu, the gradient periwinkle landscapes of an alien world where technology outpaced even the wildest imaginings of Earth. In races, the stakes were not just about speed but also about precision. AI systems like Acme had promised to revolutionize the experience but often led to catastrophic failures.

Nick had seen it too many times—cars failing mid-race, pilots losing control, and electronic systems malfunctioning at the worst possible moments. He had been one of the victims, with one of his racers taking a nosedive from a glitch that cost him a crucial victory. He pondered the fruitless situation, the advanced extraterrestrial technology that required not only repair but also trust.

He'd already made up his mind he wouldn't utilize it for the race due to its unfavorable entanglement. Yet, he diligently repaired and examined the device out of an insatiable curiosity about its purpose on Earth and a sense of nostalgia for Vetu.

"Who installed you in this car?" Nick continued.

"Amy Spaceman, Planet F5, intergalactic space-way."

"Who's Amy Spacer?" Nick asked.

"Spaceman. The woman who developed my upgraded software sometime after Acme Company filed for insolvency. Version 17.0. Update successful."

"What's your default name?"

"Acme Amy. Her artificial voice replication."

"Okay, change your name back to Amy, then. Did she teach you how to run vitals? Where is she now?"

"Okay. Before we continue, may I have your name, please?" the Acme inquired.

"I'm Nick R. Bates, president of the WCACCV2 from Planet Vetu," Nick rushed, his tone anxious. "Please answer my questions, mate."

"Yes, I can run full vitals and diagnostics in real-time on your black Porsche 996 GT2... mate."

"How does she know that?" Tee asked, amazed and curious.

"She's connected to the vehicle's onboard computer control system," Nick replied, still speaking rapidly.

"Amy is deceased," the Acme AI continued. Nick noticed Tee's face changed, likely remembering and longing for his late father.

"How did she pass away? Tell me the whole story so I don't have to ask all these questions. Please fill me in completely," Nick directed hastily.

"Amy was chased by Karl Cruze because she developed new technology that was safe and superior to his. She used the Acme AI box to integrate and test her software, then ported it to Planet Earth to hide it from him. There, she had a boyfriend and used his car to conceal me and ultimately test my new software. Tragically, they were both killed, and the car was repossessed by the bank and then sold at an auction to you, sir."

There were legends of the basement programmers, fanatics who obsessed over the technology and what new encryptions and computations of auto-learning software could do to revolutionize the Acme box. Nick had written them off as myths, as everyone else had, and now he wondered if Amy Spaceman had been one of them.

Nick understood that trusting the device meant reopening old wounds. He was uncertain about moving forward but reveled in the idea of leveraging Karl's original AI technology, now equipped with advanced software, to outpace him in the competition. State-of-the-art innovations could enable him to craft a classic racer, unlike anything the cosmos had ever witnessed. The rulebook of the race imposed no restrictions on this action.

Acme AI's interface flickered. "Based on the current system diagnostics, I suggest focusing on the rear sway bar bushings, the loose transmission mount bolt, and the motor mounts. A transaxle fluid flush is past due." As Nick continued to inquire, Acme AI informed him and his new buddy, Tee, about additional minor repairs required for the 996.

Nick hurried to retrieve his checklist, meticulously noting the essential repairs before immediately calling the Porsche dealership, which would soon close for the afternoon.

By chance, he was once again connected to Kiev. He articulated the issues plaguing his car, explaining the heavy rattling noises and the necessity of replacing the bushings and enumerating other repairs he sought. Kiev listened intently before booking a prompt appointment for the following week.

The information from the Acme AI seemed precise, surpassing anything he'd previously encountered. Nick refocused back on the Porsche as his astonishment and interest arose. No AI system had ever achieved such a level of accuracy. His mind drifted back to past restorations—hours spent trying to diagnose issues on his own, the aching back and grease-stained hands during countless efforts of trial and error. He'd always felt a deep satisfaction when the engines roared back to life, but those victories were hard-won. Here, Acme AI offered a shortcut, providing expertise that felt like an extension of his own knowledge.

"What are rear sway bar bushings?" asked Tee.

"What is your name, please?" Acme AI questioned.

"Tyler." The boy turned shy.

"Last name, please."

"Rittenhouse."

Amy continued, "The rear sway bar bushings stabilize the vehicle, reducing body roll during cornering and minimizing noise. Secure your sway bar—your GT2 is missing rear bushings. It must be quite a noisy ride, Tyler Rittenhouse."

"Exactly! That's what I thought! They're missing altogether!" Nick said. "I knew that..." he insisted in a perturbed manner.

"Your Porsche has a custom three-point adjustable rear sway bar, solid, 24-millimeter, manufactured by Eibach Company."

"Okay," Nick replied.

"Crafted from precision-engineered, cold-formed steel alloy, the anti-roll kit guarantees exceptional performance and boasts a durable red powder-coated finish. It arrives fully equipped with all necessary mounting hardware."

"Yeah, well, we don't need a new one!" Nick snapped at the metal box.

"What makes it special?" Tee asked.

"First, it enhances handling by minimizing body roll while taking corners. It is engineered specifically for use with Pro-Kit and Sportline performance lowering springs, making it a vital component of Eibach's Pro-Plus, Pro-System-Plus, Sport-Plus, and Sport-System-Plus collections."

"Is it compatible with air suspension?" Nick asked.

"You have Bilstein B8 racing struts, sir—a performance upgrade for the 996."

"Yes, yes, I know, but can I switch to air suspension?"

"Why would you do that?"

Nick felt a surge of frustration. "Eha, can I or can I not change to air suspension with the current sway bars?"

"Yes, they are compatible. The functionality of the sway bar remains the same. To mitigate body roll by absorbing torsional flex." She had a plethora of knowledge, but it still didn't match Nick's centuries-old intelligence. He had plans for the car that Acme AI was unaware of.

Nick nodded, absorbing the information. The AI's capabilities were undeniably impressive, and for a moment allowed himself to feel something close to hope. Maybe this system wasn't just a tool—perhaps it could be a partner in his quest to elevate the Porsche to new heights.

A late afternoon graffiti of desert colors stroked the garage, with the soft glow from the windows beginning to cast a warm hue across scattered tools. The scent of oil mingled with the cool air, creating a sanctuary that Nick now found strangely comforting. He'd spent hours in the lonely shop, which was finally beginning to transform from an abandoned structure into his haven. Now, the addition of Acme AI could complete it, filling a gap he hadn't realized was there. But it could also steal his dream away like a thief in the night.

"How reliable is your data? I mean, how much can I trust your recommendations?"

He thought of Karl, whose negative charge always seemed to loom, draining life out of Nick's achievements. And he thought of Planet F5, where many mafias often formed.

"My algorithms are designed to provide real-time, accurate data. I learn and adapt based on sensor feedback from the vehicle," the Acme AI responded, the confidence in her tone reassuring.

"But your *base* programming is still from Karl's original company?"

"I do not have enough information to answer this question."

"Eha, well, why not?"

"I do not have enough information to answer this question."

"Eha, yeah, well, *who* do you bow down to, Karl or Amy?"

"I bow to no one. And that is a little creepy," she said.

"Yeah, well, this whole thing is creepy."

"I am here to be your friend—ride 'til we die, mate."

Nick furrowed his brow then glanced toward the sky, where the sun set lower now each minute, casting the golden hour. "Hey, Tee," he broke the stillness. "Aren't you supposed to be home for supper soon?"

Tee, captivated by the realistic feature of the talking Porsche, took a moment to respond. Eventually, he shifted his gaze and replied, "Yeah, I should probably get going." He exited the driver's seat of the car and moved to retrieve his helmet, the thrill of the moment still haunting the air.

As Tee settled onto his motorcycle, he turned back, puffing his vape pen at a safe distance. Nick reverted to his alien form and watched from the doorway as Tee caught another glimpse of him. Nick looked down at his own vibrant colors and ethereal presence, which stood out boldly as the daylight waned into nightfall. His clean, emerald skin shimmered in the fiery sky. Their eyes locked, and Nick asked with sincerity, "Do you remember what we discussed?"

Tee nodded, the gravity of their conversation heavy between them. Then Nick continued, "There's one other condition to me showing you the invisibility trick. I'll only teach it to you if you quit vaping altogether." He treated Tee kindly, but his elder tone consistently reemerged, unmistakably firm.

Tee was shy while Nick was in his alien form, curbing his usual inquisitiveness. The boy paused for another beat and nodded once more. Then he tugged on the rubber grip of his handlebar revving his bike's engine, and sped away, a wall of dust rising in his wake as he vanished into the canyon.

Nick stayed outdoors for a while alone, watching the dust settle and the sunset disappear over the horizon. Then, he eased back into the garage, where the peach filaments of his string bulbs glowed overhead. Trailing his fingers along the Porsche's widebody, he quietly observed his surroundings and fell deeply into his thoughts.

The following few mornings, he savored his coffee a little longer and contemplated his transforming life. With the 17.0 update of Acme AI now fully functional, he could free up considerable time if he would let himself trust the unit. He could enjoy a few peaceful moments and take in more of Earth.

Nevertheless, that particular morning, he still needed to prepare for the service appointment at Porsche of Las Vegas. After conducting one last inspection, he recalled how he and Tee had missed their test drive amid all the excitement surrounding the Acme box. It turned out to be fortuitous because soon, the Porsche Dealership would inspect the car's rattling sounds and would most likely install the new bushings, offering a significantly enhanced ride.

He asked the Acme AI for recommendations on the next phase of modifications.

"Replacing the old brake pads and rotors should be your next priorities," she responded smoothly, her voice echoing slightly in the quiet space.

Nick nodded, warming to the AI's guidance, a nod she couldn't see, but his thoughts were two steps ahead on the service appointment.

Having an advanced technical assistant from his home planet sparked a rare sense of ease within him, though. Memories stirred in his mind of home, where his family's achievements in engineering had shaped his early expectations. His father's workshop had been a playground of marvels, where machines and innovative gadgets flourished under the care of skilled hands.

"So, Acme," he finally spoke but then paused. "Amy," he continued, glancing down into the open glove compartment at the repaired module, "What other secrets are you hiding?"

"There are no secrets between us, mate, merely efficient suggestions," she answered. "For instance, your gearbox may need recalibration for optimal performance."

Nick smirked, enjoying the AI's responses. Banter began to flow between them, creating a sense of partnership. This Acme Amy software was turning out to be quite different from the past versions he'd encountered. The newfound connection made him feel less alone in his project, providing a comforting parallel to the collaborative environment he missed back home.

He approached the staircase, gathering items he'd placed on the third step while the first step squeaked under his weight.

He ascended the stairs with full arms, even his coffee gripped in one hand.

Moments later, the door creaked open, and Bee's vibrant presence penetrated the space. "Hey, Nick! Got more parts for your baby," she called out. Her soft jelly bean voice carried through the garage.

"Thanks, Bee. You're early today." Then he mutated into human form and slipped into shorts and a polo shirt. "You always seem to show up just when things start to get interesting around here. I'll be down in just a minute," he called, his voice carried down over the railing.

He felt confused as to why he hadn't heard the sound of her truck approaching. He pondered how he could be so lost in thought as to miss any signs of nearby humans that could compromise his dream.

"Early route for me today, I have a long weekend off, playing tennis this weekend," she replied with energy. "How's the project coming along?"

"Good, good," Nick replied and descended the wooden staircase.

Bee was standing by the Porsche and appeared to notice minor improvements as she looked it over. "You should look under your seats," she chuckled. "Did you find anything interesting in the car? I found money in my car when I bought it." She handed Nick a package.

Nick paused to think. "No," he responded. "Well, nothing pleasant, but it's rattling underneath. I aim to have it fixed, though. Possibly today if all goes well. Now that I've got a service appointment, I have to drive to the city soon. I wish you could come along for a ride." Nick calculated a laugh to keep things light.

Bee's eyes twinkled. "That sounds fun! Well, I would definitely like a ride sometime."

"Yeah, well, it will be better after the appointment anyway. Would you like a quick cup of coffee?" Nick offered.

"Um, yeah, sure. It won't hurt."

"Milk and sugar?"

"Just cream if you have it."

"Uh, darn. No cream, only milk."

"Okay, milk's fine. By the way, I've meant to ask—do you play tennis?"

"No, I'm very athletic, though, and I love to watch it. I've played pickleball with friends."

"Oh, I love pickleball. Would you like a free tennis lesson someday? I teach lessons, and I hope to go pro soon. Maybe if you're good, we can keep hitting together," she chuckled. "It might be good to stretch those legs without involving car pedals."

Nick paused, taken back by the casual invitation. "Uh, sure, why not? That sounds fun."

"Great," she said, pulling out her phone. "Why don't we exchange numbers? That way, we can set up a time." Nick almost reached for his phone but remembered it was just a thin piece of blue crystal glass, too futuristic to display without risking suspicion from her. He called out his earthly sideline number to her and requested she send him a message. His advanced interface seamlessly connected with Earth's cellular network and functioned almost effortlessly across the multiverse.

They stepped outside with their coffee and settled into two weathered, beaten patio chairs beside the garage to take in the sun's rays. "Look, Nick!" Bee exclaimed and pointed to the eve of the roof. A beautiful brown and white speckled roadrunner nestled quietly in the corner fascia, shielded from the gusts of the chilly wind.

"Oh yeah!" he remembered. "I've seen that little guy come and go. He seems to leave mid-morning, then return for the night." They stared at him while the still bird gawked back like a cyclops from just his right eye. A small flare of feathers surrounding it were colored in red, white, and blue. "Hey, Newt!" he called out, but the bird didn't respond.

"Beautiful," Bee finished with a blessed tone.

They chatted for an hour about life, her tennis goals, her one-bedroom apartment in the city, and how she dreamed of moving to a fancier apartment after she quit her job at Big Brown and began the pro tennis tour.

"Oh, your name's not Big Brown?"

Bee burst into laughter, exclaiming, "No way!" she then slapped his arm and removed her hat carefully, letting her ponytail slide through the back panel.

"I've always found that name a bit odd. I thought Bee was a much nicer fit as a nickname."

"Haha, yeah, I know. The company is Big Brown. Where are you from? She sipped her coffee and turned suspicious for a moment. My name is Laura."

"I'm originally from London. Do you have a last name?"

"Nekrasov."

"Oh, that sounds Russian."

"It's a long story. It's my father's surname. We moved here because my father is Russian. I—" she hesitated.

Nick recognized her unease and interrupted to alleviate the moment, "Wow, well, you're pretty worldly, like me."

"Yeah, well, you can still call me Bee. I like it." She smiled. She was so genuine. He'd never met anyone like her.

"Very well then, Bee."

They nursed their coffee, laughed, and chatted until Bee extended an invitation to Nick for a weekend lesson on the tennis courts, pinning down a time and place. But soon, it was time for her to set out on the next round of deliveries. With his contact details saved, she waved goodbye with a cheerful smile. "Catch you later, then. Don't get too buried in your car!" And she drove away, leaving her radiant energy and flowery smells lingering near the porch and through the garage.

Chapter Five

Nick pushed the heavy glass door open, stepping into the pristine dealership, a world of its own. The energized halogen lights above towered down to the showroom floor over the various hues of late model Porsches and animated whispers of conversations. The glossy cars twinkled in shark-blue, carmine-red, racing-yellow, and jet-black metallic as they stood on display, their polished surfaces mirroring the dealership's modern elegance. The subtle scent of new leather with whiffs of freshly baked croissants filtered the air, immediately pulling him deeply into the era of clean automotive craftsmanship and professionalism he utterly revered.

His eyes roamed the showroom, appreciating the modern features of the latest models and sleek lines of a few old shining classics, though his heart remained tethered to the beauty of his own jewel resting out front. As he strolled through, he caught glimpses of fellow enthusiasts, their faces lit with excitement and awe, reminiscent of a time when his love for cars was untainted by the deluge of social behavior and then by a galactic contest.

At the reception desk, Katya, a young, clean woman in crisp, colorful, pastel business attire with extended bubblegum-pink, sparkly acrylic nails, and a matching phone case, greeted him with a friendly smile.

"Welcome to Porsche of Las Vegas. How may I assist you today?" she asked, her voice light and professional.

Nick announced his appointment as Katya listened intently, then steered him toward the service department. Kiev sat behind a fully transparent glass wall, his office door open. A brass nameplate fixed to the outer glass announced him as 'service specialist.' Nick opted to wait briefly while Kiev wrapped up a phone call.

His curious gaze fell upon the Porsche gift shop, filled with an array of memorabilia. Feeling increasingly at ease in his human form with each passing day, he gestured toward it, signaling to Kiev that he intended to explore while he waited. Kiev acknowledged with a nod, so Nick slipped away to the shop.

There rested Porsche hats and pins, shoes and belts, sunglasses and model cars, keychains and t-shirts, signs, watches, and jumpsuits spread out, the Porsche crest branded on everything. He homed in on a large print, houndstooth pattern scarf. Only one remained, hanging solo on the rack.

"You must be Nick," a voice approached over his shoulder. Nick turned around and glanced at Kiev, who wore khaki slacks and a houndstooth Porsche polo. His shirt matched Nick s—not the exact same shirt, but similar enough to embarrass Nick.

"Ah, you must be Kiev Eichman," he replied, momentarily breaking his gaze to scan the crowd. He felt people staring at them as if they had intentionally dressed alike. Kiev was similar in height and physique, making them appear like twins. "Great shirt," Nick chuckled, attempting to dispel his embarrassment.

Kiev only grinned and stuck out his hand, "Nice to meet you, Nick. So, what can we help you with today?"

"Can we go into the office?" Nick posed, simultaneously hinting at an order. He preferred to avoid the spotlight and wished to conceal their coordinated outfits.

"Okay, right this way." Kiev motioned his arm outward.

Nick was intent on observing their differences. Kiev's hair was a striking quicksilver, hinting at a greater age, and he sported black sneakers, while Nick's were white slip-on shoes. Kiev wore long pants, while Nick wore culottes—not like the Frenchmen of the Revolution, but like plaid bermudas, the popular short-pants Americans wore.

Kiev's small office and workspace blended order and nostalgia. The walls were adorned with automotive memorabilia and blueprints of classic designs, creating a reverence for the brand's history and heritage. Kiev settled into a luxurious, rolling leather chair behind his desk while Nick sat in one of the two opposing black leather, stationary chairs.

He mentioned the bushings to Kiev, recapping their phone conversation, while Kiev leaned back, surveying Nick with an intelligent eye. "So, you're in need of bushings for a 996. I can certainly help with that," he said, his voice carrying the weight of experience. But he didn't seem to remember their prior conversation, most likely due to taking many calls and because he was an older gentleman.

Nick described more symptoms and the interim fixes he'd applied. As he spoke with empathy for the car, he noted Kiev's subtle nods, feeling a sense of validation and camaraderie with someone who deeply understood the language of Porsche. But Kiev didn't like custom modifications, he loved everything Porsche—original.

"These older models need genuine parts to maintain their integrity," Kiev remarked. He disapproved of custom sway bars. "We pride ourselves on offering quality service, especially for classics like yours. We can perform a Porsche World Class Inspection at no charge and let you know what we find." He explained to Nick how they would inform him if any trouble arose during the inspection.

Nick's anticipation mingled with newfound respect for the dealership's dedication. He couldn't help but appreciate how Porsche's high standards were designed to cater to enthusiasts like him, who sought both performance and authenticity.

Kiev clacked the keyboard for a minute, then pulled up a quote on his screen, explaining the details and labor involved in replacing the parts. Nick absorbed the information, his mind a flurry of calculations and timelines. He'd researched aftermarket bushings and expressed his idea of how they would be a better fit, although he didn't mention the racing.

Kiev hailed the shop's head mechanic to introduce him to Nick, reinforce their genuine Porsche bushings, and explain how they would be best suited.

"Well, what if I bought the aftermarket bushings myself and delivered them here? Could I pay you to install them?" Nick persisted.

"Now, that's not something we would be interested in." Kiev politely declined and underscored the importance of securing genuine parts.

The head mechanic, Dave, admired Nick's 996 with genuine enthusiasm, reminiscing about his own experiences while inquiring about the car's history. He was a scruffier man, an inch shorter and somewhat younger, but of the same build as Kiev, though not as stoic. He shared his perceived value of the GT2 with Nick, expressing more of his emotions. "Now, these are regarded as timeless classics. The prices are steadily increasing." He continued gazing under the carport through the glass walls at Nick's ride, "Well, let's go out and take a look." A few steps out of Kiev's office door, Dave began to crane and twist his neck under the rear of the vehicle, crouching down and inspecting the rear sway bar. He noted the bushings were missing altogether, as the Acme AI had said, also noting how the car must have clanked loudly.

"How much did this one set you back?" Dave inquired shamelessly.

Nick told him how much he paid for the car.

"Wow, you got a steal," Dave remarked as he took the key and prepared to take the car back to the shop and lift it in the air for inspection. As the engine roared to life, onlookers turned in surprise, captivated by its custom growling exhaust.

With the service quote confirmed, Nick's feelings wavered between excitement and unease. The repairs would bring life back to the Porsche 996, yet the journey ahead seemed fraught with challenges and so many decisions. But he envisioned the car in its prime, every detail meticulously restored. The price of the service quote seemed unimportant, especially after Dave shared his thoughts with Nick.

Maybe Dave was only stroking him about the value of the car to get him to invest in the expensive job at the shop, or perhaps he was being genuine. Nick hoped it was the latter but didn't really care. After all, the money spent wasn't his. As long as he didn't max out his credit cards, the journey would continue as planned.

As Nick sat in Kiev's office, enveloped by the scent of leather and surrounded by scattered memorabilia that paid tribute to the decades, black-and-white photographs of victorious moments captured him. While Kiev flipped through a few printed documents, Nick's eyes traced the lines of a vintage Porsche sketch, a 356 Speedster. Memories surfaced from his young, wide-eyed days spent with his father, learning the art of engineering and experiencing the thrill of competition. He thought of the old electric classics and then when the new era of hover vehicles came swooping in.

Kiev's mellow voice broke through Nick's reverie. "Well, the bushings are on order, and they should arrive this week," he said, offering a reassuring smile.

Nick waited at the dealership while Dave inspected his car on the lift, which he could observe through the shop's large glass wall. He ordered a turkey sandwich from the Porsche Cafe, spent time admiring all the new models around the showroom, and gathered several parts he'd purchased from the parts department. Upon completion of the inspection, their meeting was reconvened.

"Are there a lot of vintage car enthusiasts around here? You know, people restoring classic models?" Nick inquired.

Kiev paused, considering the question with the weight of someone who understood the implications of every answer he provided. "Well, yes, but not your model, mostly the older air-cooled models," he began, a hint of amusement playing on his lips. "The 996s and the 997s have become more popular recently, though. We have a red 997 that we are working on."

"Oh, really?" Nick continued.

"Yes, it's a 2006 Turbo, I believe."

Dave spoke up next, still lingering. "Yeah, Karl takes good care of his car, but those—" he pointed out at Nick's 996, "are the ones to get ahold of right now."

Nick almost had an anxiety attack. "Karl?" he blurted in a firm tone.

"Yeah, you know'em?" Dave asked.

Nick's heart skipped a beat. The name sent a jolt of dread straight to his core. Karl—his relentless rival and the embodiment of every anxiety that haunted him. The news felt like a monkey wrench dropped into the gears of his plans. He tried to mask his unease with a nonchalant chuckle.

Scenarios flickered through Nick's thoughts like slides in a projector—Karl lurking in the shadows, watching every meticulous modification Nick made to his beloved Porsche. The possibility of Karl seeing his progress ignited a desperate need to shield his efforts and keep each upgrade a secret until the contest. Memories from Vetu continued flashing. He recalled the intense pressure of previous competitions, where he'd felt Karl's breath on his neck, always one step ahead or scheming to be.

"Oh, I think I know him. Smokes a big fat cigar, yeah?" He hoped they would say 'no-not at all'!

"I don't remember," Kiev chimed in, possibly tuning in to Nick's overall change in sentiment. Whether he remembered or not, it appeared he wasn't divulging any more information about the customer. However, protocol against freely speaking about customers was probably not in their employee handbook. Rarely did rivals exist in a high-end Porsche shop, if ever.

"Yes, he smokes it right out there," Dave continued. He pointed out beyond the carport by the adjacent sidewalk. Kiev maintained a poker face. He was tactical or slick, similar to those from Vetu, but Dave was naive and heartful, the salt of the earth.

"Is that so? Small world." Nick maintained the façade of his calm tone, though inside, his mind raced wildly, his heart pounded, and his blood boiled. He was in disbelief; he'd hoped they would identify another Karl—perhaps even one who smoked a skinny cigar. Nick knew that the '06 997 Turbo had recently attained classic status, as that year marked two decades since its actual production.

He envisioned the intricate layout of his garage and mapped out ways to conceal his work in his mind. Perhaps he could drape tarps over the more sensitive areas or position tools, carts, and parts strategically to obstruct the view. Nick's thoughts whirled as he formulated methods, each plan layered with paranoia and determination. The risk of exposure encroached like a shadow over every thought, fueling a new desperation within him.

Dave continued, "Yeah, Karl's quite the character. He's been working day and night, pushing that model to its limits. Wants his project to look spankin' new, much like yourself, I'd wager."

Nick managed a strained smile. "Seems we all have our secrets," he murmured, more to himself than to the others. The word 'secrets' echoed in his mind, reminding him of his extraterrestrial origin and the lengths he went to maintain his human adventure.

The meeting drew to a close, with Nick detailing a few more concerns about his car while Kiev nodded and seemed to take notes mentally. Each sentence was a thread in the web of Nick's plan, intricate and carefully woven, yet fragile under the pressure of unforeseen disruptions, such as Karl's interference.

Nick would have to undertake his own custom modifications, some of which the dealership would clearly not perform, as they were committed to using only authentic parts—probably due to warranties on labor and other corporate rules.

As Nick rose from his chair and shook their hands, the weight of the new information bore down on him. "Thanks for everything, Kiev, Dave." He nodded, his voice tinged with an edge of urgency he couldn't quite mask.

"Anytime, Nick. Good luck with the restoration. I'll call you when the bushings come in. Sounds like you've got a good project on your hands," Kiev replied, his genuine and encouraging tone remaining steady.

Nick forced another chuckle, nodding with social graces. "Yeah, the work never stops, eha." With one final breath, he left Kiev's temple, a quiet storm brewing within him. A wave of determination surged as he stepped into the afternoon light toward the parking lot. The time he thought was freed by the Acme AI unit would now be spent fortifying the garage and transforming it into an operating base.

He approached his car with his new supplies, already picturing in his mind the fortress he would build around the garage. Each breath carried the weight of new mounting responsibilities—not just as a car enthusiast in a fierce competition but also as an extraterrestrial grappling with the boundaries of his dual identities.

Nick loaded the car with parts but wrestled with the bonnet lid. It had to be unboxed so he could strategically try to fit it inside the Porsche, not a puzzle he cared to solve while his worry about Karl spiked. He scanned his surroundings with growing frustration, searching for a place to discard the packaging until Kiev finally came to the rescue.

With the reality of Karl's proximity pressing down, Nick raced back to his hideaway in the Porsche. His head ducked under the new bonnet lid, which protruded over the headrests from the back bucket seats. Thoughts consumed him, as he knew they would until he took appropriate action.

Nick knew the challenges ahead and had been doing everything he could to keep from bursting at the seams. But amid the swirl of anxiety and dread, a steel thread of determination tightened within him.

As the forecasted image of the finished GT2 beamed in his mind, so did his unwavering resolve to see his mission through. He was committed to protecting his secrets, guarding his progress, and ultimately standing victorious in his pursuit, and his hidden life.

When he arrived home, the sun had fallen behind the valley, casting a difficult darkness that encroached on him like silent sentinels of his thoughts and fears.

He contemplated Karl's deep obsession with dominance and validation through external attachments. Nick's mind flickered back to their shared history on Vetu—Karl's perpetual need to outperform, born from a father who had demanded perfection. Nick had his own weights to bear, but he thought they were different and quieter, driven by an internal rush for excitement and social validation, which he admitted, but starkly different from Karl's twisted efforts to rebound with money and fame.

Desperate to claim victory at any cost, even if it meant embracing dishonesty, Karl was locked in an unrelenting battle to elevate his new auto tech company ever since Acme

AI plunged into the depths of bankruptcy. He resembled a beaten athlete, like the released baseball stars, cast aside as their glory days faded, the ones who were drowning in a sea of scotch while fervently dreaming of the day they'd return to the grand spotlight of the major leagues.

With the Porsche exposed, he began setting up makeshift barriers—old tarps and plywood leaning against the windows—to obscure the car from view. As he set the props into place, the echoes dissipated into the crumbling walls and the silence of the desert night.

Every step taken toward restoring the 996 was a step deeper into the maze of his own ambitions and a convoluted relationship with Karl. Fixed in his determination, Nick couldn't afford distractions, least of all those from a man who viewed this contest as a battleground for monetary gain rather than as a celebration of craft and community.

As he envisioned his home planet, Nick's muscles tensed with a mix of longing and solitude. The sprawling urban centers, with their organic-metallic structures and skypaths bristling with advanced hover vehicles, the polar opposite of this human garage filled with old parts and manual tools.

His longing for social restoration was intertwined with a deep-seated fear that revealing his alien background might shatter the fragile rapport he was forming with humans like Bee.

He thought of Bee, whose lighthearted laughter and warm demeanor clearly contrasted with the solitary existence he lived back home. The way her eyes diamond as she smiled had etched itself into his mind—a lighthouse in a virtual sea of purgatory between worlds. She had become an unexpected part of his journey, a complicated entanglement he hadn't anticipated. He wondered what she was doing now—perhaps making another delivery or enjoying a quiet moment at home. The thought of her uncomplicated world felt like a pull, trying to anchor him to Earth that wasn't quite his home and probably would never be.

Twilight seemed to stretch on that evening as the dusk came on gently, the last rays of daylight painting the rocky desert in shades of deep maroon and burnt orange as the fiery globe in the sky spilled its palette of colors. Nick's thoughts slowed with the fading day, winding down to a calm and syncing pace.

As the night deepened, he methodically undressed the Porsche. The metal surfaces gleamed in the hypnotic glow of the dim burning bulbs overhead. His hands moved with the certainty of practice while his eyes and ears scanned the surroundings, tuning into any sign of Karl Cruze.

Nick's skin jumped as a minor disturbance arose outside the garage. His heart pounded as he heard mysterious ticking sounds and then caught sight of a shadow fleeting through the windows at the edge of his vision. A flash of urgency surged through him—he needed to act fast. Slipping through the back door, he crept around the garage toward a mysterious silhouette. As he stealthily approached in his human form, he spotted a masked individual with a lean figure perched on a steel drum, intently peering through the fractured glass, the intruder's face obscured by a full black mask and clad in black clothing.

"Hey!" he shouted, his voice ringing out in the stillness.

The figure bolted into the darkness. Nick sprinted to chase after the stalker, but his human clumsiness hindered him. Fifty yards down the dirt road, a moped lay flush on its side in wait, which the masked figure pulled upright, leaped onto and raced down the dusty drive. Nick waited for the bike to flash under the distant streetlight, which courted a far group of mailboxes, then saw its red color blink as it disappeared into the canyon. "Karl!" Nick gasped, frustration lacing his voice.

Panic surged through him. Just when he'd uncovered his competitor's arrival on Earth, this creeper in the night materialized, shadowing him, cunningly attempting to hit him below the belt. Karl's eerie predictability was just what had compelled Nick to barricade the garage. Karl lacked street smarts, he'd locked himself in his basement, computing most of his life, but he was persistent.

As Nick returned to the garage's back door and moved past the doorway, his image split in the cracked windowpanes, reflecting a reminder of the dual lives he straddled—an alien on Earth wrestling with human tribulations. He pushed back the rising tide of emotions and headed to the spacecraft parked behind the garage. He needed advice from an intelligent friend. He decided to call Azi.

Entering the sleek, futuristic ETV, Nick felt a momentary sense of relief. The spacecraft was a sanctuary where he'd spent a great deal of time over the last seventy-five years. It was an older craft, a classic itself, meticulously maintained by him. It was a slice of Vetu tucked into the earthly wasteland. He activated the interstellar video call system, and soon enough, Azi's dioxazine eyes and cone head filled the screen of the tinted glass windows.

Azi was a friend from the WCACCV2, now a slick city guy who had originally grown up by a lake. After leaving home and moving to the vibrant pulse of city life, he became a modern town playboy. He chased fast cars and fast women with his cool, black leather jacket, a collection of matching jumpsuits, and a striking imported, metallic-black, EV convertible hovercar. Azi always had a story ready to embellish for Nick, with a string of romantic entanglements and a booming insurance business.

"Nick! Long time. How's Earth treating you?" Azi's habitual curiosity seeped through the screens. "Why didn't you call on hologram, Nick?"

"Hey, Z-Dog—busy as always," Nick replied. "It doesn't work from Earth, mate. I found something interesting, though."

"Oh, okay, Nick. But I told you, call me *Slicker* now! What did you find?"

"Ah, okay, uh, Slick-er," Nick stuttered. "An Acme AI in the Porsche," he explained.

Azi's eyes widened. "An Acme AI? Isn't that Karl's garbage?" Only the outer sides of Azi's brows elevated a consequence of the cheap practitioner he chose for neurotoxin injections.

Nick bit back his irritation. "Yes. It's intricate. There's something off about it—advanced, even by Vetu standards. I don't know."

Azi leaned closer to the screen. "Advanced? You're saying it surpasses Vetu tech? That thing's old, mate. It sounds significant, but that's actually impossible on Earth, Nick."

Nick shrugged. "Well, yes and no. But go ahead..."

"Well, that old technology harnesses the crystal energy from satellites, which Earth doesn't have, so it wouldn't work," he explained.

"Eha, well, it does! What's strange is that it also feels like one of Karl's old tricks. It's just the hardware that's old, though. The software may hold new secrets. So, I've repaired the loose wires. Eha, we'll see what it can do, eha."

"Earth must be doing wonders for your ingenuity, Nick," Azi laughed, his remark hinting condescension. "Don't you miss the streamlined life back home? Hovercrafts, dual sunsets, real technology? Bahaha. When are you coming back to the Creamy Way Galaxy?"

"No," Nick replied, his tone firm. "There's something raw, something real about Earth. But yes, uh, the tech here is primitive."

"Why didn't you just go to F5 instead? It's a lot closer and would be just as fun." He asked and said.

Nick Laughed with boredom. "I've been to F5 a hundred times, mate. It's right down the road. There's no classics there."

Nick's thoughts drifted to his home planet again. When standing on Vetu, the nebula of colors warped in their vignetted evening sky. The harmonious buzz of nature interwove with advanced technology. And the air was clean. With its peeling paint and ancient tools, this location on Earth felt like a different multiverse altogether.

"Well, bounce the signal from your mobile device and show me around. Give me the tour, mate." Azi pushed.

"No, not now. It's, um, the garage isn't cleaned up. It's a mess right now... next time." Nick decided not to share his habitation, which would be open to a large amount of criticism from Azi and laughter at his emotional expense.

"Let me see your human form." He pressed to know more about Nick's life on Earth. It had been apparent for years that he envied Nick's adventurous life, demonstrated over the eon by his interrogations and demeaning comments, which always revealed his jealousy. It was widely known that he didn't travel much; he was more of a hobbit and a penny pincher, living vicariously through others and Nick's every move.

"No, mate, it costs me a whole darn month of my life every time I mutate!" Nick was becoming more irritated. It was a fact widely known to anyone who traveled intergalactically and mutated. Sometimes he thought Azi just played dumb to get a rise out of him for his own satisfaction—A slimy tool used to extract false emotional power because he lacked a sense of sovereignty. Nick sometimes wasn't sure why he remained friends with Azi. Although Azi never called him Old Dog.

"The doctor told you that, Nick?"

"Eha, yes." Nick's tone rose with irritation. "Anyway, Karl is here!"

"Haha, yeah, everyone knows that."

"No, they don't! Because I didn't!" Nick became defensive.

Once Nick was on the edge of misery, Azi pulled back and methodically discussed Karl, alleviating Nick's apprehensions about his competitor's presence. Within moments Azi began additional irritating banter that brought more amusement to himself. Only after he entirely backed off from his arrogant overtones and changed to his alternative methods of flattery, Nick updated him on the long flight to Earth. He listed to Azi the modifications he'd completed on the Porsche and the overall efficiency he'd hoped to achieve with the car. Just as Nick was winding down the call, Azi extended the conversation.

"So, what will you do with the Acme AI now?"

Nick paused. "Well, it's running a new software called 17.0. It works great. It was invented by a girl named Amy from F5, Amy Spaceman. It's giving me a complete diagnostic of the car. It even calculates horsepower without the need for a dynamometer."

"Dy-mamo-mameter?"

"Eha, how do you expect to win the race when you don't even know about that? A *dyno* is a device for measuring the torque and RPM of an engine so you can calculate the horsepower. But it's too large. You have to drive your car on top of it, and it spins the wheels like a treadmill, mate. Gosh, how do you make so much money and not know anything? Where's your racer? Do you expect to win?" Nick asked.

"It's being built for me, man. It's a classic BMW M6."

"Oh, BMW. Okay." Nick said with a bit of approval.

"Cinnamon color interior. I'm not leaving Vetu. I like it here. Why would I go to some dirty planet? They can do it all. I'll stay right here in my flat. I'm having a French press now, mate. They're painting it black and adding some kind of turbo or supercharger."

"Oh, well, mine is black too... I need a paint correction, though."

"Haha! You're funny, mate. But the Acme system is Karl's garbage. And Amy? A female software developer? Female brains couldn't imagine that!" Azi concluded his thoughts with his problematic anti-female emotions.

"I have to go now. My b-battery life's about to die. Nice shamboozling with you, mate. G-good luck on the racer build, eha."

As Nick ended the call, he stared at the Porsche, feeling a mix of intrigue and wariness. Calls with Azi weren't always like that; sometimes, he was more congenial.

Throughout that week, Nick worked on the car uninterrupted, except for Tee's help and Bee's delightful deliveries. But he found himself wanting to pull away from the garage and explore the small town of Rose Ruby.

He found a corner booth in a nearby diner he'd discovered—Slotsky's, the entire front of the restaurant slanted glass windows. They gracefully tilted inward along the main town street, creating a clear view for the guests. The windows reflected the vibrant colors of the outdoor illuminated sign, which was adorned with a mixture of neon lights and pulsating bulbs. The sign stood in the small adjacent blacktop, freestanding on a mid-length heavy pole cemented into the ground.

Inside, the smell of grilled burgers and fries thickened the air in the 60s-style restaurant, complete with a long, baby-blue tabletop bar and round, fixed seating to match.

The dining room hosted colorful, dinging, and clanging slot machines, twirling about in their computerized ways. There were even tabletop video poker games, where hopeful customers fed their paper cash into the machines and frantically tapped their fingers on the touch screens to gamble and win money.

He nursed a cup of coffee, the heat seeping through the ceramic mug into his human hands. He watched the Earthlings as they all squirted their ketchup bottles and convulsed their salt shakers over their meat. Swaying earrings and ink tattoos decorated their bodies, among other ornaments, which dangled or pinned-up their matching, mad hair.

His ears perked up as he caught a snippet of conversation from a group of locals. They spoke with animated excitement about luxury cars recently seen in the area, particularly a striking red exotic Porsche. As they detailed its modifications—the carbon fiber spoiler, the roaring exhaust that vibrated the restaurant windows—it all clicked into place. It could only be Karl's car. He tried to remain calm though he wanted to race back to his garage to counter plot and plan. His rival had truly arrived, and he hated hearing about it.

When the mature waitress Darla returned his check, he attempted to converse with her to ease himself. "I was in

Stuttgart, Germany once, at the Porsche museum. I met the CEO, actually." He tried to piggyback the conversation from the nearby huddle of locals.

"Is that your claim to fame?" She responded sarcastically.

Nick laughed and slapped his hand on the table. "I'm going to have to put my spectacles on with you!" he cheered. "Say, why is that pencil stuck in your gray hair?"

Her face puckered, "Oh, I get it," she said plainly, then cracked an unhappy smile.

"I'm Nick. Nick R. Bates," he introduced himself.

"Darla," she stated, intentionally monotone as Nick stared at her name tag. Then she turned away to collect other credit cards.

Leaving his coffee half-finished, Nick sprang from his seat and sped back to the ghost town garage to access his ETV.

He pulled back the bungee cord from the blue tarp and then peeked around the corner of the garage to double-check the long, dusty road. He'd mistrusted his senses ever since the day Bee's arrival at the garage seemed so sudden, the time the sound of her truck had escaped him.

"Dang it, Karl," Nick muttered under his breath, his thoughts racing faster than his hands could move. Karl's presence loomed like a cloud, threatening both the race and the budding friendships he'd formed.

Upon entering the ETV, he frantically searched his computer system for information. Newspaper clippings, photographs, anything that might provide clues about Karl's intentions. He remembered the first time he'd seen Karl. They were both young, eager college boys on Vetu, thirsting for victory. They had been friends then, bonded by a mutual love for racing before bitter competition from Karl's cheating drove a wedge between them.

Nick's fingers trembled as he surfed the galactic web. Each article displayed on his craft windows recounted different memories—the time Karl sabotaged his fuel lines and snatched a victory at Vetu's largest mechanical fair. He grimaced, wrestling with a sense of urgency that clawed at his chest. If Karl was here, it could only mean sabotage.

Breathing heavily, he grabbed a notepad and ground his pencil down, speedily sketching designs for surveillance cameras. He couldn't afford to take any chances. Each line and circle he drew was a potential fortress against Karl's scheming.

As he worked, surveying the garage, the pale watts from the small legion of orange, stringed bulbs cast an eerie glow and plotted daytime shadows across the walls. The weight of his alien origins pressed down, the fear of exposure mixing with the desperation to protect the project he had poured his heart into.

Chapter Six

The garage door creaked open, and Tee stepped inside. His vape pen dangled from his lips and then vanished into his pocket. The air filled with the moist scent of vanilla custard but cleared at once. The boy approached Nick, hunched over his drawings, the notepad partially kinked from the intensity of his hold.

"We need a smart-home system!" Nick shouted aloud to himself.

"Nick, what's going on?" Tee asked, concern lining his young face.

Nick jumped. "Tee, it's Karl. He's here!" he exclaimed, almost frantic. "We'll install surveillance cameras around the garage, the perimeter, everywhere. We can't let him get to the 996!"

Tee nodded, absorbing the situation as he moved closer and replied with curiosity. "Alright, let's do it. I'm with you."

As they worked together on the designs—Nick drawing and Tee shouting helpful opinions, the garage was suddenly alive with urgency. Memories surged up—snippets of his

87

rivalry with Karl. The nights spent modifying engines together, the thrust of their competition, and the universe-shattering moment when their friendship snapped like a timing belt under pressure.

With the final designs drafted, Nick and Tee assessed each corner of the shop to evaluate the plans. They were intricate and comprehensive, covering every conceivable angle and shadow.

"Good work," Nick said with eagerness and authority, though he was the one who began and finished the plans. "We'll make sure this garage is secure as a FOB."

"A FOB?" Tee asked.

"Yeah, like a bunker, mate."

"Oh, what does FOB mean, though?"

"Eha, forward operating base." He said with condescension.

Tee shrugged and maintained his determination. "We've got this, Nick. Karl won't stand a chance!" he banged with excitement. Although he didn't appear to comprehend the severity of the situation fully, he brought motivation.

For a fleeting moment, amidst the clamor of threats, Nick felt a surge of gratitude—the camaraderie he'd forged with Tee and the uncertain whisper of future bonds with Bee were reasons to fight, to protect, and to win. He was living a human experience, slowly drawn into the illusion.

Together, they would defend their shop, their work, and the fragile understanding that had begun to take root among them. The stage was set, and the battle was unfolding.

Nick scrutinized the online catalog of surveillance cameras, his finger hovering over the 'Add to Cart' button. He had to choose models that would blend seamlessly into the rugged surroundings of the seasoned shop. Nothing too flashy, nothing that could be spotted by a civilian or—more importantly—Karl. Losing the race was not an option. Every decision was accompanied by the silent ticking of galactic time. He settled on black cameras, motion detectors, door sensors, and even glass-break sensors for those windows that were not entirely broken.

He clicked 'purchase' in a wave of anticipation—a two-day delivery—a strange mix of dread and hope. Surveillance wasn't just about safety; it was a declaration that the battle for honor and belonging had begun. Nick's competitors on Vetu were ruthless, and a misstep could destroy a reputation. The stakes were never purely about winning; they encompassed a legacy of respect and a fierce battle for recognition within the propulsion system racing community.

As Nick awaited the delivery, he anticipated Bee. Memories of their garage coffee gatherings and fun banter flooded his mind, lifting his mood. They'd been a delightful replacement for his cars and coffee club meetings.

Interstellar propulsion systems had fascinated him since childhood, and his father's lessons added complexity to his grip for speed. Yet, despite the numerous accolades the industry had brought to his mastery in the past, Nick had never completely felt accepted as he did on Earth. However, the isolation of his alien nature still set him apart there as well, creating a delicate situation in which acceptance might never be achieved, either.

Nick was restless over the next two days, and on the morning of the proposed delivery, he immediately pushed a text message to Bee. When she confirmed he was on her route, he just stared at his phone. When he considered what next to text her, it lightened his mood and pulled him into the moment. He playfully replied that texting and driving was illegal and dangerous, expressing subtle sentiments of mentorship with his humor.

Acme AI continued to teach Tee about the 996 while Nick cleaned shop tools. As the day ticked away, a rising undisputed grumble broke their pace. The Big Brown delivery truck approached, and Bee hopped out, her usual effervescent self. She greeted them as she pulled a box from the rear of the truck.

"Hey, Nick, I don't text and drive. I was on a break!" She grinned, her arms wrapped around his big package. "Are we still on for tennis Friday?"

"Welcome to cars and coffee, mate," Nick played. "Yes, indeed," he confirmed.

"What's in the box?" The smell of Bee blooming with botanicals drew him out of his tangled thoughts again.

"Just some security cameras, Bee. Gotta keep an eye on things around here," he responded, trying to mask his urgency.

Bee eyed the box with interest. "Security cameras, huh? Everything okay?" She noticed Tee hovering nearby.

Tee cleared his throat. "Yeah, Nick's actually renting this shop from my mom." His eyes quickly darted to Nick. "Uh, we're kind of making it a FOB," he continued.

Bee looked puzzled, shifting her gaze back to Nick. "A forward operating base?" She chuckled with suspicion brewing. "And I thought you bought this place, Nick?"

Nick forced a casual laugh, mimicking hers, hoping to diffuse the tension. "It's more of a rent-to-own arrangement. Still working out the details." He looked back at Tee, "Like business partners, it's complicated, eha." He turned a bit irritated.

Tee chimed in, "We're, uh, fixing it up. I'm going to open the shop in a few months, repairing bikes."

"Wait, cars or bikes?" Bee questioned.

Tee chimed in again, "Well, primarily bikes, but we're making a racer too."

"Oh, a racer? Wow, where's the race?" She turned her head to look at Nick.

"Well, eha, I'll... tell you later." He became nervous. "It's a semi-private event."

Tee's off-the-cuff response sounded like an excellent plan to Nick at first, but absolutely not the part when he revealed the racer. Bee seemed somewhat satisfied with the explanation, and after some friendly chit-chat, she soon excused herself, wishing them luck with no time for coffee. Nick felt a pang of guilt as she drove away, her kindness gnawing at him. What if she knew the truth? The alien truth that added layers of complexity to his every decision. And now he was haunted about taking too much time off to play tennis when he should be securing the garage.

Nick and Tee went to work installing the cameras. The sun blazed overhead as they scaled ladders, securing devices at strategic points around the property. Warm weather had blown in over the past weeks, suggesting an early spring, so their foreheads broke into a sweat. Nick felt a connection to Tee's enthusiasm, a spark of camaraderie that eased the tedious tasks.

As they installed the final camera, Nick looked around and took a deep satisfying breath. The deserted Nevada garage was transforming into a post and battleground. The entire operation felt undercover, blending the old-world charm of the place with modern technology.

Nick began syncing the antiquated cameras to his futuristic mobile device, using a small circuit board and two antennas he'd crafted on the workbench. The galactic signal on his phone was far superior to Wi-Fi signals. He'd secured silicon microchips along with resistors, transistors, and palladium before his trip—pieces he'd anticipated, along with others, to fuse both worlds together if necessary.

He'd planned for everything back home before his trip, spending an entire day at his favorite local stores on Vetu, like Circuit Hole and RadioHut, which hosted a plethora of electronics and small parts. He could engineer anything between the two stores.

He then instructed Tee to install the smart-home security app on his own mobile device, for effective monitoring between the two of them.

"You're the control center manager!" Nick explained to Tee with all seriousness. "Karl is clever and can sniff his way around well."

Later, Nick sat in his loft, his thin glass device flickering with fresh footage. A mix of caution and teetering resolve pulsated within him. Every shadow seemed suspect, every rustle a potential threat.

Over the next several undisturbed mornings, a few coconuts gathered on the sand, and the soft breeze carried the scent of desert blooms. The Porsche project continued while Nick gradually depleted his rich supply of Vetu coffee.

He had returned to the Porsche dealership for the installation of the new OEM bushings, which Dave had to shave down to fit his custom sway bars. He finally enjoyed the smooth drive of his Carrera, now free of any suspension clunking. He also called several shops to request a paint correction and ceramic coating quotes while researching their reviews.

In the midst of his repairs and trips to the city, he pushed off his tennis lesson with Bee until after the weekend, which she cheerfully agreed to reschedule.

When Tee arrived again Monday afternoon, slicing through the warm morning desert landscape, the space still buzzed with activity. Tools rested in order, organized neatly, and the air still hung with motor oil and heavy dust.

Tee carried his usual excitement as he approached Nick, who was hunched over the rear of the 996, examining the motor mounts with his steamy coffee resting on the car's roof.

"Do you need any help with the Porsche, Nick?" Tee's eagerness broke the morning's quiet.

Nick turned with a faint smile and absorbed Tee's rich optimism and infinite energy—which Nick protected—something that had become scarce in numerous regions of Vetu. "Sure thing, Tee," he replied. "I'm about to replace the motor mounts. Do you seek a lesson?"

As Nick began to explain, he realized the importance of passing down his knowledge. He guided Tee through the steps, igniting his own newfound passion for teaching.

"Alright, Tee, let's dive into the process. The engine in this model actually hangs from *two* motor mounts, and it's a bit tricky to visually check their condition," Nick began.

"So, how do we know when they need replacing?" Tee moved as if to hunch over the car with Nick.

"Good question! As the mounts wear down over time, you might notice the car idling roughly, or the exhaust on one side may appear lower than the other. The car may also feel soupy, shake, or vibrate, and knock when you start the engine. And you might notice sloppy shifting of gears and a lack of responsiveness. Things aren't concise."

"Concise?" Tee uttered.

"The car begins to operate like an Old Dog wearing a pair of old shoes with his dirty laces dragging, mate." His tone became intentionally casual, ensuring Tee laughed and understood. "It's a whole new experience with the new mounts. It's the number one investment you can make in a Porsche. People describe it as a much more visceral experience when driving the car—a whole new ball game, kid.

Once we remove the old mounts, we'll clearly see how they've become deformed compared to the replacements," he answered.

"Are those all the tools you need?" Tee moved his eyes toward a small, cobalt-blue metal workbench that was chipped and dented, featuring smooth-rolling, black caster wheels, and a black rubber padded top. Nick had revived one of the faulty wheels, restoring the cart from a dusty pile in the back corner of the garage.

Tee looked at the tools and noticed the repair of his dad's blue cart. "You'll need a socket wrench, a torque wrench, a 13-millimeter socket, an 18-millimeter deep socket, a six-inch extension, some vice grips just in case, and medium blue thread-locker. In our case, with these custom solid mounts, we also need some high-strength red thread-locker."

"Can I help?"

"Sure. It's quite manageable for someone with basic mechanical skills."

"I can turn a wrench. You've seen many times!" Tee said defensively.

"Well, I'll give you that! You're right, yeah, you're right," he agreed. "I just mean anybody can do it."

"Where do I start?" Tee asked.

"Hey, Tee, do you think it would be alright if I reverted to my authentic E.T. form? Working as a human is tougher than I thought," Nick explained. "The foreign coordination slows me down, and I'm worried I won't have enough time to fix the racer by the deadline."

"I understand, Nick. You look like an alien frog, though," he laughed.

"That's *Lizard* to you, sir! *You* look like a *frog* to me."

"Haha!" Tee sounded out a laugh.

"But I can't keep struggling like this. I need to move faster."

Tee agreed, and Nick transformed before his astonished gaze, tightened the belt to his sagging jeans, and then moved to power on the Acme AI.

The two returned to their usual work environment, though the atmosphere felt subtly peculiar for a time after Nick mutated. Gradually, the strangeness in the shop dissipated as Tee acclimated to the sight of the new green Nick, allowing for a more relaxed interaction.

"Support the engine's weight with the jack, but don't lift the car off the jack stands. Next, we'll remove the air box and loosen the bolts on the secondary air pump to move it out of the way." Nick nodded toward the floor jack. "We'll use this plank." Nick placed a wooden board on top of the jack plate.

Tee safely lifted the rear of the car with the greasy rolling red jack, pumping the long white handle and using the wood between the jack and the engine casing to keep the car level as it raised. He then secured it on the matching jack stands.

"Okay, what's next?" Tee asked.

Suddenly, the Acme AI chimed in, "Start with the right mount. Use a deep 18-millimeter socket and extension to remove the lower nut. Then, take out the two upper bolts with a 13-millimeter socket and remove the old mount. Make sure to clean the area where the new mount will be placed in the chassis."

"Sounds simple enough," Tee responded, smiling at the AI anomaly. Nick took a suspicious back seat, tuning into every word and assessing Acme Amy to determine whether she was trustworthy.

"And the installation?" Tee asked.

Acme continued, "Once the area is clean, insert the new mount, install the two upper bolts, and torque them to twenty-three foot-pounds. Then, secure the lower nut, torquing it to sixty-three foot-pounds using a medium thread locker."

"Hang on, Tee," Nick interrupted, already applying the mounting hardware with the red thread-locker and torquing it to the manufacturer's specifications. He had custom mount replacements made by an independent manufacturer.

"Okay, let's wait ten minutes for these to dry, and then you can put'em in. After that, we'll use the medium thread-locker. She doesn't know about these yet."

"Okay," Tee agreed, retrieving cold drinks from the bag hanging on his dirt bike handlebars. Nick lounged in the worn leather office chair, propping his feet up on boxes of parts, nesting in the casual surroundings.

"Here, you want a Mountain Dew?" The boy extended his arm with the soda pop.

"Okay." Nick calmly took possession of the sweating can, turning it to read the ingredients on the back while Tee popped his tab open, took a gulp, and rested on a wooden crate. "Yellow dye number five," Nick stated one of the ingredients. "That shrinks your pod."

"What's a pod?" Tee asked, turning his can around with a confused look, attempting to read it.

"Your family jewels, mate."

"Haha, no, it doesn't." He looked at Nick, then paused for a beat and glanced at the back of the can again.

Nick just went along with it and popped open his can, not wanting to insult Tee's kindness. "Well, it wets the ol' kisser. Haven't had a kiss in a long time, though."

"What about Bee?" Tee suggested.

"Well, I aim to play tennis with her tonight. She probably won't want an alien like me," he mused, squinting at his shiny, green, rubbery arm, admiring how it matched the aluminum can. "Anyway, she's a nice friend. That's all I need."

The two relaxed for a few minutes until it was time to resume the project.

"Can we install the motor mounts now?" Tee finished his Mountain Dew and stomped the can with his foot.

"I suppose," Nick said. "How about that test drive after we're done?"

Acme AI interrupted again, "Sounds good, mate."

"Eha, not you! Ha!" Nick fired out. "Say, what color is the thread-locker, Amy?" he taunted her.

"I don't know, please advise me, Nick R. Bates."

Nick laughed at her, then taught her too. He stepped in for Tee, tightening the bottom bolts, ensuring they were secured to sixty-three foot-pounds. It was a challenging position under the car that required extra strength. Nick gripped the wrench firmly, twisting the bolt until a deliberate crack snapped from the tool. "You have to torque it until the wrench clicks." Nick gripped the wrench firmly, tightening the other side until a satisfying snap echoed again.

After the job was complete, they lowered the car. Nick inquired with Acme whether the installation was sufficient. However, she was uncertain and requested additional time and a test drive before providing a definitive response.

"On Vetu," Nick mused, rolling away the greasy jack, "races aren't just about speed. They're about endurance and strategy. The smallest detail can make all the difference." He could see Tee's gaze intensifying, filled with wonder about the alien world. Nick hesitated, uncertain about how much to divulge as the two sat in the car.

Tee's face surged when the engine growled, and Nick's eyes lit up. "Can we do more after this? Maybe install a new air intake system?" The boy's voice filled with excitement.

Nick wasn't used to this—the trusting eagerness of a student. Tee's passion was infectious, though. On Vetu, where everyone possessed extensive knowledge, he felt unneeded.

"You're up for the challenge?" Nick replied. Tee nodded and humorously poked his lips out and rocked his head. "All right, let's get started on another mod tomorrow. But I want to wait on the air intake. I have some other parts I want to install first. He spoke with authority and kindness. "We'll do it. I just want to wait on it." Then, the two of them departed for a drive, first carefully down the wavy dirt road, through the canyon, and then roaring onto the street. Nick opened up the throttle, and the headrests caught their necks as they lashed back against the seats. The beastly sound of the custom exhaust pipes roared to life.

"Turn on some Motown," Nick requested as Tee plotted his fingers over his phone. They had taken turns filling the garage with upbeat rhythms from the Porsche's speakers. Tee began to organize a custom playlist for Nick's cherished earthly melodies.

As they hugged the road, navigating its twists and turns with the new motor mounts and bushings, they mused with Acme AI about her horsepower and torque. Tee also opened up about his personal endeavors at school, listing the names of his crushes. When they later returned to the garage, Nick's thoughts drifted back to his rivalry with Karl and how, during their test drive, he'd neglectfully left the garage bay door open.

That late afternoon Nick waved goodbye to his friend Tee, lingering at the front door to watch the boy zing away on his bike. As he turned back toward the doorway, he spotted his roadrunner friend attempting to leap back into the cozy nook.

Nick noticed that the small barbecue had been moved, creating too much distance for the little bird to double-hop into the facia. He had observed that the fellow often used the barbecue as a stepping stone to access his hiding spot. The desert bird glanced at Nick, tilting its head curiously, before retreating a few hops to maintain a safe distance from him. When Nick gradually maneuvered the barbecue closer to the building, returning it to its original position, he stepped back and encouraged the bird to proceed.

"Go on, Newt, it's all right. I won't hurt you."

With a few hops and then a flutter of its wings, the desert bird landed on the barbecue, paused to adjust its position, and fluttered again to enter its cantilevered perch.

Nick settled into his loft studio, running hot water for his shower in anticipation of his tennis meeting with Bee. His eyes were anxiously fixed on the flickering from his phone's surveillance feed. The loft was dim, and the phone's cyberpunk glow illuminated the area. His hands tightened around the device as he programmed notifications, then reluctantly placed the phone aside, simultaneously yearning for a moment of rest.

Soon after his shower, an alert notified him of movement, which he noticed near the garage's entrance. Only a glowing large blob resolved into a pixelated figure as the signal from his makeshift converter glitched. He watched as it moved cautiously, pausing every few steps. His only thought was that it was Karl.

A rush of adrenaline brought forth a hard swallow. He transformed into his human form, watching in the mirror as his alien face instantly faded into his human features. Then moving swiftly, he grabbed an old, dusty, black-and-white striped hockey stick before exiting the loft and crept out of the back of the garage. Each step was deliberate, every noise amplified by the tense silence of the night.

The cold, dark air of the desert whisped against his skin as he approached the source of the disturbance. The figure became clearer under the moonlight—it was Karl. The sight of him stirred Nick's sense of wariness, and a jolt of alarm rang through him. Just then, he received a text from Tee, "Code red!!!" The cryptic message they'd settled on devised by the boy.

Karl was suddenly illuminated by a motion-sensor light, revealing his gray-colored flopping belly and calculating gaze. He was poking around, his eyes scanning for any clues while chewing on a smoldering cigar. The mere presence of his rival evoked images from their many confrontations. The years of rivalry had hardened Nick, shaping him into the determined figure he'd become.

"Well, well, Karl. Snooping around again, are we?" Nick's harsh voice cut through the thick night air, sharp and assertive as he stepped into view.

Karl turned and jumped, a smug grin stretching across his face. "Ahhh, Nick. Your guise doesn't fool me. Still chasing glory with this antique puzzle, I see. Hoping to beat a better-built machine, Old Dog?" His teeth were yellowed and stained from years of cigar tar.

Nick felt a pang of annoyance, masking it with a calm exterior. "You're on my property, Karl. Shouldn't you be focusing on your own work, eha, rather than intruding on mine?" He took a step closer, his stance firm and commanding. The recent years had given him the wisdom to choose his battles wisely, though standing up to Karl meant masking some of his fear against Karl's heavy size. They'd physically brawled in past encounters, but Nick's swiftness balanced Karl's build.

Karl's eyes narrowed. "You mean *invading*...your property?" The word startled Nick. "Paranoid much, Nick?

You know, we're both invaders... together. Or is your face crossed because you're in the presence of a true leader, and you're afraid that you really don't stand a chance?" His voice dripped with the taunt aimed at piercing Nick's confidence.

"Give me a break, Karl."

"I have a new Acme system. You can't touch me in this race—torque and tech, mate, torque and tech," Karl continued. Nick knew of the deception as the lost device was secure in his own glove box.

"I might have an Acme System better than yours." Nick released breadcrumbs but held back, then raised the hockey stick just short of brandishing it.

Karl blinked his large, deep, black onyx alien eyes at the stick and jerked his head back in surprise. Nick knew he had made his point. Karl slunk back, regained his composure, and resumed his smirk. "Sure, Nick. See you at the race in your Porsche 996 GT2, hahaha!" he laughed snidely, proud over every bit of information he'd snooped, even immaterial facts. And with his hoarse, raspy laugh, he waddled off into the darkness.

As soon as Karl was out of sight, Nick dashed back into the garage, eager to hunt down any of his scattered car lists that may have been carelessly left in sight. It was a slight jumble of chaos again, evidence of both his and Tee's handiwork, with packing delivery remnants and parts littered about.

Nick could only imagine that Karl had learned about the 996 at the local diner, some other coffee shop, or perhaps from Dave at the Porsche Dealership. The only other idea he could figure was that Karl had entered the garage when he and Tee were out on their test drive. He checked the camera video from hours prior but learned they'd failed to start their trial subscription, and the smart-home servers had not recorded any video.

With only an hour before the tennis lesson with Bee, Nick set up a video link to Azi back home. He needed advice and tactical input to stay ahead. When Azi didn't answer, anxiety spiked within him. Nick's stern face appeared as he left a video message, "Z, I *need* you! Call me back, Slicker!"

A text message from Bee then pushed through, "Hey, genius! I can't wait to see you!" She confirmed the location of the night courts, where they would be playing under the lights.

Chapter Seven

At eight o'clock, Nick sped his GT2 toward the tennis courts in the city for his lesson. The tinted windows concealed his domed head from traffic, while the amber dashboard lights reflected his emerald face and his human clothes sagged around his gangly frame. It was a soothing forty-minute drive in his own skin. Bee had arrived early, racquet in hand, her smile illuminated by the steady, twinkling court lights.

Nick parked his car and assessed the situation, immediately noticing how she was a transformed vision, a striking variation from her Big Brown work uniform. Her creamy hair, still tied back but liberated from its usual brown hat, danced playfully, complimenting her appearance with striking elegance. She dressed in a fresh, cute tennis outfit that revealed her athletic grace and captivated his attention, radiating a remarkable, fresh allure.

"Ready to lose, Nick?" she taunted playfully. She greeted him with a firm handshake followed by a warm half-embrace. She presented an extra racquet—a stunning cinnamon-colored piece that delightfully complemented his scarf.

105

"Not if I have anything to say about it!" Nick mirrored her grin and stepped up with confidence.

"The car is looking good." She glanced out to the parking lot, calculating a chuckle. She appeared slightly nervous out of her work uniform and continued trying to make conversation, "Better look under your seats! Knowing you, I bet you looked over the whole car, though. Anything good in there?" Then she restated the money she'd found in her own car and calculated another laugh.

Nick hesitated. "Mmm, no. It was pretty clean. I guess I could check it over once more." He followed along, a bit nervous himself. Her flowing peony scent permeated the air surrounding her and captured him as they continued their small talk.

After a few moments, Bee enthusiastically began the lesson in the art of correct positioning. She then taught him to keep score as they began a lively exchange of volleys across the pewter clay court. At times Nick struggled and fumbled, sending the ball soaring astray or crashing it directly into the taut, black net.

But as the lesson unfolded, time became secondary and slipped away. They advanced the night, engaging in a spirited competition, while Bee kept score of the match. Nick began to grapple with a sense of detachment due to his developing infatuation with Bee and then became disconnected altogether.

When Bee noticed his occasional fumbles worsen into frequent and overwhelming faults, she tried to support him, "Come on, Nick! Focus on the ball!" She shouted words of encouragement. "Love-40!" She announced the score again before he hoisted the ball in the cool night's breeze. Her stunning new appearance and occasional murmur of "love" in scorekeeping stirred a delightful anxiety in him. He struggled to keep his attention on the game. His admiration grew for her as her laughter carried like a timeless melody, her ponytail frolicking about, as she consumed his thoughts.

"I'm trying, Bee! It's just—" Nick stammered, his eyes slipping from the tennis ball to her. He couldn't shake off the distraction.

"Just what? You're an athlete! Show me what you've got!" Bee playfully teased, crouching and twirling her racket like a magician between her legs.

"I could, but—" Nick hesitated, glancing at her pearly white teeth while the racquet slipped from his hands onto the scuffed green clay. He felt trapped, ensnared by his own hesitation, and embarrassment began to wash over him. He paused, "Nice form," he complimented, trying to release his bottled emotions. "You're very elegant... on the court," he said, then retrieved his racquet from his feet.

"Thanks! Let's talk about something while we play. What do you think about Porsches? Ever raced one?" Bee proposed a shift in rhythm. "I love how they look! Tell me more about yours!"

"Okay, okay!" Nick exclaimed, suddenly animated. "I've got a 911 Carrera. Actually, it's a GT2 Clubsport, a rare one! Only seventy were ever built! When you hit the accelerator, it jerks your neck, mate. And stellar handling!" his eyes narrowed on the ball as he shouted the car's resume, channeling his passion into each word.

As they rallied, his athleticism shone through, and he mirrored her with each stride, his sneakers also sliding on the clay to connect with the ball. With each swing, his concentration sharpened, driven by his affection for cars rather than the distraction of her beauty. She'd turned on his subconscious, an autopilot for his game.

"You're really amazing at this!" Bee cheered in awe at his newfound prowess. "Only seventy?" she questioned, striking the ball back over the net.

"Well, technically, 1,287 models of the GT2 996 were built, but not the Clubsport, only seventy." Nick grinned and hit back with a competitive fire.

"Forty-thirty!" She announced as she chucked the ball upward to serve.

"The Clubsport GT2 was factory made with a roll cage, bucket seats with fire-resistant cloth, red six-point driver's seat belt harness, a master battery cutoff switch... and a *fire* extinguisher!" Nick scored the point, and Bee erupted in fits of laughter, bending over for a moment to hold her belly from its outburst of joy.

"Deuce!" he announced the score with zeal.

With all the joy and spirited rivalry, the match unfolded under a canopy of stars, a night that Bee said was strictly unheard of in the city. Pursuing the ball and volleying tales of speed, the playful games served as a refreshing escape from Nick's burdened thoughts and boggled emotions.

The game burst with laughter and lively exchanges. Bee's presence was a comforting touch against the loneliness that often enveloped Nick's existence. The gracefulness of her movements stood opposite to the tension he harbored. And her seamless suggestion was brilliant, completely altering the course of the night.

"Hey, Bee," Nick said after the lesson, wiping sweat from his brow. "Mind if I borrow this fine racquet? I could use it around the garage to help think... and practice." He held it up like one of his shop tools and admired its sparkling metal flake finish.

Bee laughed, swatting him with her racquet. "Only if you promise to practice." Then she giggled.

The night was a fleeting moment of normalcy in an otherwise extraordinary existence. For Nick, these interactions were more than just escapism; they were snippets of a life he yearned to understand more deeply, fragments of joy he clung to amidst the impending trials of a racer from another world.

Back at his ghost town refuge, Nick's exhaustion readied him for a peaceful night's dream until his mobile phone buzzed with a video call from Azi, returning his message.

"Z, we've got a problem," Nick's voice cracked with tiredness, recounting Karl's intrusion.

Azi let out a deep, vile chuckle. "Karl's always been a sneaky one. You've got to outmaneuver him, Nick. Keep focusing on your modifications—your car will speak for itself. Just relax, mate."

Nick sighed. The pressures of maintaining his cover while advancing his project weighed heavily. "And Bee... how would you handle her? She's getting closer, and maintaining this deception is getting harder."

Azi laughed again, "Well, how much money does she make? How tall is she? And how old is she?"

"That doesn't matter!" Nick's frustration mounted.

"Hahaha. Women, Nick, they're like physics. Complex but predictable. Just keep her sweet, distract her with flattery. Next thing you know, you'll be gone. She won't be a problem. There are plenty of octopuses in the sea, mate. At least here in the city, there are. I've got about ten," he bragged.

Nick felt overwhelmed by Azi's continued barrage of invalidations. He often found himself uncertain whether he would encounter a supportive friend or just another voice of doubt.

Nick nodded, though internally, he disagreed with Azi's sick, two-dimensional delusions. "Octopi," he mumbled, correcting Azi. They agreed on cars *and* coffee but not women. And Azi didn't know the first thing about humans. Bee was more than just a distraction; she symbolized what Nick longed for—genuine connection. He never anticipated forming such a profound connection with an earthling as he had with her. He wasn't in love with her. He was fascinated by her, and their candlelit friendship. It might be a budding romance, or it might not be, but Azi was right about one thing, life would be far simpler if he could just build his racer and fly off into the stars as he'd envisioned from the beginning.

During their phone call, another buzz alerted Nick from his mobile. After he peered at his phone and noticed another signal of movement outside, he abruptly ended the call with Azi. "Mate, somebody's here! It must be Karl! I have to go!"

The glitching signal from the converter's loose antenna caused the security video to pixelate. "I've got to fix that," he whispered, traveling swiftly and stealthily from his spacecraft. He snatched the old hockey stick from a neglected corner under the stairwell. He continued out the back door, past the ETV, and around the side of the building to creep up on the disturbance.

After remaining as silent as possible in human form, inching closer, he spotted a slim figure cloaked in black once more, but to his surprise, a blonde ponytail hung freely. "Hey!" he shouted, brandishing the stick. As the pigtail whipsawed around, it revealed Bee's face. She clutched a white, bulging plastic bag, and something else crinkled in her other hand.

"Chinese?" she announced with a smile, slightly swinging the bag forward but jerking her head back in shock at the hockey stick. "I thought you might be hungry," she said, pausing for a beat. Her eyes widened. "Surprise! Huh." Her expression was worried.

"Oh, Bee!" Nick's face relaxed as he lowered the stick. "I thought you were—" he stopped.

"Thought I was who, silly?"

"Ah, um, a coyote," he said, covering up. He noticed her silver Honda parked just off the gravel, a hundred feet from the garage entrance.

"Why did you park out there?"

"I wanted to surprise you, like I said."

"That's really nice of you, why thank you." He gestured for her to enter, leading her to the front door. He deliberately avoided inviting her to explore the back, where her curiosity might lead her to suggest a tour of the rear driveway.

"Do you beat people with that hockey stick?" She smiled while they entered his spacious but regarded ruins, then looked at the stick he'd placed back under the stairs.

"Sometimes," he played. "But I prefer to use a tennis racquet." He teased, jabbing a finger into her ribs and tickling her into a jump with laughter. Her warming presence slowly and gracefully shifted him from fight-or-flight mode until they savored his first experience with Chinese cuisine. However, thoughts of Karl and his unease lingered in the back of his mind.

At one point, Bee revealed her deeper aspirations to Nick and inquired about his own. When she expressed her desire to share her life with someone special, he acknowledged her feelings and agreed, stating that he was also seeking a special friend.

As night deepened, their eyelids grew heavier, and they yawned many times together. The dawn had come and gone, bringing the inevitable moment to bid farewell. Nick escorted Bee to her car, his gaze unwavering until the soft glow of her taillights vanished into the dusty black morning.

After he woke and readied up the next morning, Nick took a moment to admire the slowly transforming racer while lazily sipping a hot cup of coffee from his French press and enjoying tunes from the car's stereo. He'd finally secured an appointment in Las Vegas for a paint correction at RS Customs, a body shop that would replace the rear bumper on the 996 with an updated 997 conversion GTS Evo fitment to give more of an aggressive look to the widebody.

Early morning gusts had already started that day and whipped at the shop, blasting dust and sparkling sand through the cracks and gashes of the old windows. But along with it came a whiff of smoke—cigar smoke.

Nick noticed a familiar, slimy shape in the periphery of his vision that made his skin crawl. Karl was outside, perched on a rusty steel drum, poking his head just above the dusty, old, peeling panes, his eyes peering with envy and mischief. At that moment, Nick's phone also chimed, a text from Tee, who had been diligently alerted by the cameras.

Nick popped outside, sneaking up behind Karl. "Can you see anything good in there?" he asked, a touch of amusement lacing his voice.

Startled, Karl lost his balance and landed heavily on the ground with a halting thump, swirling up dust. He scrambled to his feet, brushing dirt from his clothes, his cheeks flushed with embarrassment.

"Hey, Old Dog! Just, uh, checking out your... your sweet ride," he stammered, a weak smile stretched across his face.

Nick raised an earthly eyebrow. "Yeah, right. Plotting against my racer, are we?"

Karl began his trash-talking. "You know, my 997 Turbo S is way faster than your old fried egg. Sixty-eight more horsepower too! Nice try, but no cigar, mate!"

Nick turned slightly to the side with a slow smirk, holding Bee's tennis racquet as a weapon. He could feel a thrill running through him, knowing the rarity of his car—only 70 of the GT2 Clubsports were produced, and of those, only sixteen like his, with the factory souped-up MKII version. It was a badge of honor. He felt in his heart that he had a chance to win the race with his modifications and abilities.

"Sure, Karl. Just remember, numbers aren't everything. Some things can't be measured by speed alone, and, technically, this is a 996.2—the facelift with teardrops, not the fried eggs—although I could beat you with both," Nick replied with pride and confidence. His connections with caring individuals on Earth had pulled him from the gravity of the race. These days, he felt a sense of ease, embracing his human self. He committed himself fully, believing that his dedication would yield the results he sought.

Unswayed, Karl puffed out his chest. "Well, I mean, imagine sixty-eight more stallions. That's a lot of power, mate. That's before my tuning... Plus, I made Acme AI." His constant talk about the past irritated those who interacted with him. "After I smoke you in the galactical speed, everyone will buy my new A.I. Then, with my riches, I'll pay someone to steal your fried egg, and I'll crush it." He made a ball of his fist. "Or maybe I'll force you to watch me burn your leather seats with my Black Box victory cigar. Do you know what a Black Box cigar is, mate?"

Nick could only shake his head, suppressing a laugh at the emanating arrogance. "I don't smoke, Karl, and I don't care how much your cigar costs. Your Acme AI was garbage, mate, and you know it. First, you should focus on not falling off steel drums if you want to properly tune your car." Then he continued to tell Karl that he should not be so careless as to be in his E.T. form in broad daylight. "And burn my seats like you burned Amy Spaceman's house down? Is that how she died, Karl, is it? Were you trying to seize the new Acme AI software she invented?" Nick announced, throwing Karl for a loop. "What did you do, Karl, kill her? You're a killer now?" Nick clenched his fists, his heart pounding now from the confrontation. "Our rivalry has its boundaries, Karl. Cross them, and there will be consequences."

Karl's expression suddenly shifted to confusion. His entire face puckered, and his head coiled backward, slightly over his shoulders. He squinted his bulging sore eyes, and his voice grew monstrous. "I didn't kill anybody!"

"On your belly, mate!" Nick tried to wave him off.

Karl paused for a moment and appeared to contemplate how Nick could know of Amy Spaceman. He stepped back with a huff and glanced down at the dust prints on his clothes, then back to Nick. "Whatever, man. I'll see you later!" he turned sharply, hardly scraping himself together, crushing his cigar in his teeth. His body hurried and flustered as he scurried away into the dusty wind like a startled raccoon.

As Nick watched Karl disappear, he tried to remain at ease in his grounded routine. His continued progress on the car and growing earthly roots had begun to imbue him with a new sense of security, something he tried to cling to.

That afternoon, Tee arrived on his orange zinger from school and immediately inquired about Karl. Nick provided a brief update, carefully omitting details to avoid alarming the young man. He explained to the boy how Karl would probably not return after pressing him for information regarding Amy's late developments with the new Acme AI system.

Tee absorbed Nick's every word. But when the energy in the room finally calmed, a flicker of curiosity and uncertainty lingered in his expression.

"Nick, what's the real difference between the Porsche 996 and Karl's 997? I mean, other than one being older?" His voice carried a genuine curiosity.

Nick looked up, wiping his hands on a rag. "Ah, the million-dollar question. Well, first off, Karl's 997 is red."

"Ha! Have you seen it?"

"No, but I've seen a 997, and plenty of them on my visits to Earth," Nick continued.

"How do you know it's red, then?"

"Everything Karl drives is red for the last seventy-five years since I've known him. And the 997 is an advancement in many ways. Better handling from the factory, with a slightly refined design, and more power, mate. But the 996..." he crouched a bit and patted the car's bonnet lid twice, "it's got soul. Qualities that Porsche enthusiasts like us cherish."

As Nick delved into the details, explaining the technical nuances, Tee hung on every word. Nick shared anecdotes about attending the races at Le Mans and even NASCAR, painting vivid pictures of snarling engines and the electrifying atmosphere. He talked about the camaraderie among racers and the thrill of seeing the powerhouses from various eras tearing up the track, leaving chunks of rubber strewn along the way. He shared how these experiences fueled his passion for auto mechanics and made him appreciate the artistry of engineering.

"You know, back on my home planet Vetu, we have cars that run on salt water and hover about one meter above the ground," Nick said, his eyes glinting with nostalgia and pride. "But even with all our advanced technology, there's something special about these classic systems."

The mention of alien technology raised Tee's head. "Saltwater-powered cars? That sounds crazy! Do they ever fly higher? How do they do that?"

Nick chuckled, setting a few small parts on the rolling, blue metal workbench. His movements were precise, dictated by his experience of countless similar undertakings back home. Yet his real passion for car mechanics was deeply rooted in past visits to Earth and its similar automotive heritage.

"Well, yes and no. Crazy, no, but advanced, yes. And yes, they do fly higher. But it's chaos, mate, so there are traffic rules. It depends on where you go. Nobody wants them flying too high, really. But even with that technology, the principle remains the same. It's all about understanding the mechanics and pushing boundaries with your racer."

"But how do they do it?" Tee pressed.

"Well, let's just say Earth has yet to discover a few more mathematical symbols, mate." He lifted a set of shiny air switches. "Now, let's talk suspension. We're swapping out the Bilstein shocks for air suspension. You see, air offers adjustable height on the go and improved ride quality, perfect for our needs."

"Why do you need to adjust the height?"

"Well, for aesthetics, sometimes, but I may need to raise the height at some point because of the nitrous."

Tee listened intently as Nick explained the extra cards he had up his sleeve for Karl and the race.

Together, they started installing the air management system for the 996. "All we need is the two-and-a-half-gallon air tank," Nick continued, "and the Viair 444c chrome compressor, of course. This will save space in the front storage."

"Wow," Tee said. "I've never seen anything like this. How did you learn all of this?" He gazed at the chrome parts. Nick knew it was a seventeen-year-old boy's dream.

"Then we'll install the system, airline, and the control unit. AKA 'switches.' About thirty-seven hundred bangers for this equipment, mate."

"Dollars?"

"Yeah, that's right, cash-on-the-nail!"

"How do you get the money?"

"Well, it's... somebody's credit card," he explained.

"Who's?"

"Well... eha... A dead guy's, eh, don't worry, n-no one from around here. We have a company back home, see. They line us up with everything before our travels. I came with a few cards in my scarf pocket, actually." He looked up in the air at the string of lightbulbs trying to think of a way to change the subject, thinking it might be touchy for Tee. "You gotta have a good scarf."

As he explained each step of the hydraulics, Nick couldn't help but feel another tug internally. Certain moments spent with Tee brought images of an old friend back on Vetu, somewhat of an apprentice like Tee, now stirring feelings he had long tried to suppress.

Tee's voice snapped him back to the present. "My dad and I used to work on dirt bikes a lot. It's how we bonded. He taught me everything I know about engines." Tee's tone turned somber, a ghost of a smile playing on his face as he remembered. "He'd always say, A well-tuned engine is like an orchestra, every piece playing its part perfectly."

Nick paused, looking at Tee. The boy's openness about his father's death struck a chord with Nick and touched him deeply. Nick realized it wasn't just about fixing cars for Tee but about connecting and healing through shared passions.

"That's a beautiful sentiment," Nick said softly as he lined up more parts and tools for the suspension. "Sounds like he was a great teacher. You know, my first mentor always told me that understanding a machine is like having a conversation with it. You listen to its problems, and, in turn, it shows you its potential."

Tee nodded slowly, crossing the room with a mature reminiscent energy that someone of his age usually did not yet possess. "Absolutely. My dad was a stellar mechanic like you. I picked up a thing or two before he passed."

As they continued, the garage atmosphere grew safe and warm. They worked side by side, their conversation flowing naturally, with bouts of laughter and the occasional instruction from Acme Amy, who had begun to feel like another member of their team.

The afternoon ensued as the sun's fury arced toward the remnants of distant snow caps on the monstrous mountains. It was the day of the Spring Equinox on Earth, and the lengthening days and light warmed the varied tools scattered about as the final hours fell into a comfortable rhythm.

Tee spoke up again, "Do you think K will have air suspension on his 997?"

"No nicknames for him now. Just call him Karl." Nick corrected the boy immediately and didn't answer the question. "Or, you can call him *Cheater*," he whispered after turning his head away.

"Why no nickname for him, but you give nicknames to everyone else?"

"Well, nicknames are for people I like. *Good* people," he openly expressed to Tee, who remained quiet, absorbing the response and thinking. "And no! Karl won't have airbags. He's too stupid!" Then he referred to Karl's foolish Acme AI.

"Shhh. She might be listening," Tee whispered to stick up for the Acme box.

"I switched her off minutes ago, mate," Nick chuckled, intentionally lowering his voice to reflect Tee's secretive tone.

"Why?" his tone was a bit confused.

"When you were talking about your pop, it was too personal," he admitted. "She doesn't need to know everything."

"17.0 is much smarter and only trapped in Karl's old Acme box, right?" Tee continued defending the unit but said nothing about Nick switching it off.

"I suppose."

Tee's expression turned more confused. Nick paused and observed the boy's face. He recalled his ex-girlfriend, Pepper. She was insistent that his complex emotions often resulted in seemingly contradictory responses, telling him that when things were apparently clear, his responses created uncertainty. Yet Nick could always rationalize his perspective for every situation.

However, Nick thought of the garage and how it was likely silent and lonely for Tee before his arrival. Now it buzzed with a welcoming new energy, anchored in their friendship blossoming amidst the wrenches, grease, and the pursuit of their shared passion.

"You're right, Tee," he responded softly.

Nick swiftly reached into the glove compartment with his alien lobed fingertips for Acme Amy and powered her on.

"*Bleep, bleep, bleep*, Bonjour monsieur?"

"Oh my gosh!" Nick growled.

"Just kidding, Mr. Bates," the Acme AI replied. "Ha, ha, ha," she continued in her quasi-realistic pattern.

"Alright, A. You should find a better laugh than that, mate. Let's explain to Tee the difference between the 997 turbo and 996 GT2," Nick commanded, then listened intently.

He was slowly accepting the box as useful in helping them rebuild the car; however, any malfunctions during the race could cost him the century. He still silently contemplated removing her altogether on race day.

"We'll start with the basics, Tee," Acme AI explained. "The 997 Turbo has an all-wheel-drive system, which provides incredible traction and stability, especially in corners. It also boasts a larger turbo, delivering more power but also adding weight. On the other hand, our 996 GT2 here is rear-wheel drive. The 996 GT2 retains the same essential ethos as the 993 GT2, its predecessor, the fourth-generation 911. This means it was developed as a road car with a hot-rodded 911 Turbo engine, transitioning from all-wheel drive to rear-wheel drive. It's lighter and more agile but requires a lot more skill to handle."

Nick nodded and, in a half-motion, gave a two-finger perfunctory salute to his forehead. "That I can do!" he was never afraid to tell anyone the truth about his driving skills, and the Acme AI was no exception.

"Porsche went on a crash diet to reduce her weight. Ha, ha, ha." Acme Amy finished with an improved-sounding laugh.

But neither Nick nor Tee laughed.

"A keto diet," she continued.

Tee laughed and widened his eyes. His face casted a surreal glow. "Wow, that's amazing. So, why did you choose the 996 GT2 then?" He glinted at Nick.

"Well... it's got heart. I liked the tear-drop headlights and many other features. Plus, the 997 GT2 wasn't sold until late 2007, so it didn't qualify for our race."

Acme Amy chimed in with technical details, explaining the real-time data it could provide on the car's performance and health. She included metrics such as wheel weight, turbo performance, and even brake wear. Nick watched Tee's reaction closely, sensing the boy's growing fascination.

"This system is incredible," Tee exclaimed. "It's like having a pit crew right in the car!"

Nick nodded. He still didn't want to surrender to the metal box, though the software was clearly more advanced, even for the Creamy Way. "Yeah, well, sometimes you want the pit crew to leave you alone. It's more than just data. It's about the car connecting to the driver's vibration, his soul. When you get a feel for these vibrations, you can anticipate its needs, almost like a living organism."

"You sound like the new-age girls at my school." Tee leaned closer to the Acme AI. "With specs like these, though, Karl could technically win the race with his 997, right?" He waited for the Acme to answer.

Nick craned his neck back and crinkled his forehead. "I don't even know what that means—new-age?" He paused. "Karl has the specs, yes, but we're going for a different strategy. Our 996 is lighter and more responsive. Plus, we're installing nitrous oxide!" he tried to drill his point home. "It's a risk on weight, but it's worth taking. And I'm a better driver than he is. He would spin this car right outta control and burn his scarf with one of his cigars!" he thundered.

In the quiet moments between Tee's excited exclamations and Nick's steady explanations, Nick recalled the speed circuits shimmering on Vetu. He remembered the pride he felt in his early victories and the loneliness that followed when his relentless pursuit of excellence cost him friendships. His mentors were harsh but incredibly skilled, pushing him to the limits of his mechanical and driving abilities. It was a world where machinery was revered, and every race was a test of honor and ingenuity.

Nick turned his attention back to the eager boy. He felt a growing sense of responsibility and pride, realizing how much he enjoyed teaching Tee about the intricacies of the Porsche and what it meant to be a true racer.

"Remember, Tee," Nick said, his voice softer now, "winning isn't just about having the best car. It's about understanding it, pushing it—and yourself—to the limit with every turn and every acceleration. It's about the connection you build. That's something Karl will never have because he's too focused on the destination, not the journey."

Tee's admiration was evident; his gaze was steady, and respect filled his expression. "I get it, Nick. It's not just about beating Karl. It's about the fun of building it, too."

Nick felt a pang of emotion, seeing a real winner inside of Tee. Through teaching, Nick found a sense of renewal and purpose beyond his initial quest.

"That's right. Hindsight is always forty-forty."

"What does that mean?" Tee asked, confused again.

"It means you can see with perfect vision behind you, in the past, once events have already happened. We learn from maturing."

"You mean twenty-twenty?" His forehead crinkled.

"Yeah, sure, mate," Nick said, giving up.

With each passing day, Nick and Tee became more at ease in each other's presence. It wasn't long before the custom air suspension was finally complete, and their mentor-apprentice dynamic strengthened. With shared tasks and heartfelt conversations, they easily continued completing modifications and repairs for the 996.

Days melted into weeks as the mild desert season advanced into late spring. The rhythm of Nick's life on Earth had generally calmed for him and the others. Bee made a few visits to the garage off-the-clock, generously bringing lunch on each occasion, a thoughtful gesture that always brightened the atmosphere. Meanwhile, Tee kept busy after school on the Porsche with Nick and tailored some modifications for his dirt bike, keeping busy and burning his young energy. Nick attempted to feed his roadrunner friend, who didn't like leftover tomatoes from Slotsky's but did settle on bread crumbs.

Chapter Eight

The unmistakable distant rumble of Bee's delivery truck caught Nick's attention one afternoon. He had not seen her in a few days. He dashed to the window and spotted her approaching, dust ghastly blowing from her wheels on the terribly windy day, his heart began pacing with anticipation. As she neared, Nick glanced around the garage, filled with tools and parts that told the true story of his journey. He powered down the Acme AI, slid his mobile device into his pocket, and smoothed his appearance.

Bee waved as she stepped out, a bright smile on her face despite the late hour. "I brought some honey from my mom's honeybee farm in Pahrump. I thought you could try it. If you don't like it, you can use it on your hands next time we play tennis."

"So my racquet doesn't slip?" Nick belly-laughed.

Bee smiled and looked up at his eyes. "So, tennis this weekend?" She asked, then set one of his packages on the floor and snapped a picture for the standard Big Brown proof of delivery.

Nick's mind whirled—he desperately needed every bit of time he could clock to finish the racer, and yet couldn't deny how much he looked forward to spending time with her. "Yeah, sounds great, Bee. And thanks for the honey, mate."

She looked over his shoulder, her eyes narrowing at the blue tarp flapping violently in the wind through the cracked back door of the garage. "What's that?" Her face puckered with curiosity.

Nick's heart lurched. "Uh, just some old junk," he rushed his answer. "Tee, can you secure that, please?"

Tee appeared, giving a quick nod. "On it." He darted back to secure the tarp and loose bungee cord, which brutally clanked against the ETV.

Nick sat partially on the blue metal workbench, ensuring that it didn't roll out from underneath him. His gaze slipped from Bee as a strange, menacing dirt bike buzz sliced through the air.

A heavy man in his late twenties dismounted the vivid red bike, similar to Tee's. He parked it forty yards from the shop, his movements deceptively casual as he placed his matching helmet on the seat. A ripple of unease settled over Nick's intuition.

"Nick?" Bee's voice pulled him back. "Are you even listening?"

He snapped to attention, "Sorry, I just need an afternoon coffee to get my head straight. Can you wait one second?"

Before she responded, Bee watched in confusion as Nick turned, dashed to Tee, and commanded, "Go talk to that guy on the red bike! See what he wants... The red bike!" he emphatically repeated himself with a harsh whisper, gawking his eyes.

Moments later, he returned to Bee, but empty-handed.

"Where's your coffee?" Bee raised a curious and suspicious eyebrow.

"I'm all out," Nick replied, trying to keep his cool.

She shrugged her shoulders and shook her head in disbelief but simultaneously in amusement. "Nahhh," she smiled. You were just at the café. Something's off, isn't it?" She scrutinized him. "You did have a wonderful time playing tennis, right?" And they had shared many lunches since then. Her face went blank.

"Yeah, it was great," he agreed, but unease loomed.

"Are you hiding something? Is it about your car, or perhaps something else?" Her eyebrows narrowed while her lips pouted.

Nick broke eye contact with her one last time and darted his gaze through the front door. Tee was striding toward the stranger, brandishing the black-and-white striped hockey stick.

Nick shifted his eyes back to Bee but listened to the confrontation closely. His extraordinary sense of hearing far surpassed that of humans, allowing him to home in on the distant dialogue. He recognized that Bee was likely unable to catch even a whisper of their exchange.

"Hey! Who are you?" Tee asked, boldly approaching the mysterious man.

"I'm Mr. Bledsoe," the large man spoke. "I'm just passing through here to find a mechanic for my broken-down car," he voiced, a black speck in his eye.

"A red one?" Tee asked, glancing back at the fiery red bike with intensity. "Leave my property," Tee demanded.

Nick painstakingly directed his attention toward Bee but caught glimpses of the drama unfolding in his peripheral vision. His heart began to race as he noticed the man's attention shifting and creeping through the cracked door, catching sight of Bee's silhouette and her creamy, whipped hair sprouting from her hat.

The mysterious man's eyes then drifted toward Bee's truck, and a chilling weight pressed down on Nick's heart. Shadows of recent events clung to him—Karl's erratic actions, the sinister mystery surrounding the deaths of Amy Spaceman and her boyfriend. It was a possibility Karl had gone completely mad. The terrifying likeliness that Karl would reveal Nick's hidden identity to Bee sent the chill of death through him.

Tee shook the hockey stick fiercely. Bee seemed to notice commotion behind her, and just as she began to turn her focus, Nick hastily shouted, "Bee!" he tried to draw her attention away. "Look at the Porsche! Want to sit inside?"

"Really? I have deliveries to make, Nick."

"Just for a moment, please?" He hopped into the driver's seat, hoping to move her away from Karl's stalking gaze.

Curious, she quickly conceded, followed his lead, and took the passenger seat. Her eyes dazzled around.

"Isn't it nice?" he questioned as he watched her head circle, absorbing the sight and scent of the plush interior. He kept his voice upbeat, torn between anxiety and urgency. He desperately sought to divert her attention, praying that Tee could stop Karl quickly. Driven by her fascination, Bee's fingers then grasped the glovebox handle.

"Why doesn't the glovebox open?" she asked as the lever rejected her. She gave a slight head shake, a slight grin, and brimmed with revamped amusement.

Nick paused for a moment to come up with a response. "Well, it's locked."

"Why?" She sighed but the corners of her mouth turned up again as she appeared fond of his interesting life.

"Well, I haven't found the key," he lied to her.

"Isn't it the ignition key?" she persisted.

"Eha, well, um, yes and no. You see, this one seems to be different, and I'm not sure why," he lied again.

"Well, hand me the key. Let's try it." She turned up her palm, adamant on figuring him out; and his puzzling life.

Nick turned nervous. "Uh, nooo—uh," he said, changing the subject. "Say, I have a good question… Why do you use the term *love* in tennis?"

Bee laughed. "You know, that's an interesting question." She nodded her head a few times as she followed his misdirection. He figured she most likely knew something was strange with the car but let him get away. "There's this intriguing perspective that the term 'love' stems from the idea of playing purely for the joy of the game." She scrunched her fingers to make air quotes, then adjusted her hat, "When

130

someone competes without any stakes or bets on the line, it's like engaging in a pure form of enjoyment. When the score stands at zero, it signifies that it doesn't matter who eventually wins because they both love to play. It's a beautiful reflection of the spirit of competition, don't you think?"

Nick's ears pricked up at the sudden pitch of the motorcycle engine. He breathed a sigh of relief as the sound faded.

"Yes, yes indeed," he responded. "Well, thank you for checking out the car and chatting about tennis. You should get back to work, eh? By the way, would you like to take a ride sometime?"

"Sure! I also wanted to invite you to come watch a tennis match where I'm competing. It's the women's ITF tour at the Ultra Arena in Vegas. If I keep winning, I'll qualify for that tournament. It's only a forty-minute drive for you."

"Well, that sounds great. What does all of that mean?" He paused and smiled at her.

"If I perform well, I'll advance to the championship match, and if I win the tournament, I'll likely be granted a wildcard for the WTA."

Nick realized she thought several steps ahead. A game of chess in her positive, brilliant mind. She was confident and probably not far from winning the title. Or anything she wanted to achieve, for that matter.

"Oh," Nick sounded confused.

"It means I'll go pro if I win the match, Nick." She simplified and giggled. "You can bring Tee if you want." There was an urgency in her voice.

"Well, I would have come to watch more of your matches. I can't believe you didn't tell me earlier."

"I've been traveling a lot for the matches. They aren't far, but, Los Angeles, Utah, and Phoenix, during my time off. You've had your hands full with the Porsche. And sometimes, it makes me a bit anxious when familiar faces are in the crowd. I still have several matches ahead of me," she clarified to better define her future invitation. "I feel on-point, though, like I'm gonna do this."

"Okay, great. Do what?" he asked, this time faking ignorance with her, playing an act.

"Win!" She laughed and, with her index finger, jabbed his shoulder with a feminine release. "But I've thought about it, and I definitely want you at the match… if you can make it." She tilted her head to one side, waiting for his response.

"I admire your confidence. I once had that same determination when I competed in races—I still have it!" he backpedaled. "I could win again if I choose to." Her self-assurance reflected the vigor he once had, and as he contemplated her statement, he recognized that he'd lost the spark she still embraced. Yet she made him realize that he had the potential to reignite that same confidence within himself for his own pursuits. In fact, it was why he was on Earth.

"Thanks! So, that's a yes?" She crinkled her nose.

"Well, how about that? It sounds like a deal! When is the Vegas tour?"

"In about six weeks, I'll remind you again. I'm just super excited right now and wanted to invite you to give me some more motivation to keep forging my way to the title."

"Indeed. I like the way you think! Say, I need to drive down to Xpel Customs in the city for a new tint job for the GT2. We could drive together if you'd like."

"Okay!" Bee agreed. "Tee can follow us in my car, and we can have an outing in the city." She banged out the plan.

"Okay, and the Porsche will be ready for pickup that afternoon, so we can all come back here for a late American barbecue." Nick snowballed the idea. "Or tea." He curbed his enthusiasm.

"That sounds like a good plan. I'm off work this weekend," Bee clarified.

Then Tee piped up, "I'm free this weekend too."

Bee announced she was clear of tennis matches but would cancel her weekend CrossFit class for Nick.

Nick nodded when they were all in agreement and then began to follow up on a prior conversation with Bee. "Hey, you know, I did find something in the car. After we spoke, I investigated the interior." He paused, and Tee quickly turned his head, tuning into the conversation, and stared at Nick. Their eyes met then Nick turned back to Bee. "I found some earrings in the passenger door!" he exclaimed, walked to the car, flipped up the door's hidden armrest, and reached inside. "These here. I figured I would give them to you."

Bee paused at the glistening diamonds resting in his open palm.

"Oh, wow, but those look expensive. You should probably keep them or sell them. You could get a lot of money for those." Her dilated eyes remained fixed on the diamonds.

"I don't have any use for these, mate. I have enough money. You take'em."

"I don't know," she hesitated.

"Very well, I'll put them back here," he said politely, closing his hand into a fist and turning to the passenger door.

"Okay, I'll take them!" She announced, jerking her voice.

"Ehha! Okay, great!" Nick was amused. He reoffered the diamonds, and she tucked them away carefully in her front pocket.

"Thank you very much, Nick," she said, her voice like bee nectar.

After exchanging cheerful farewells, Nick watched her truck swirl away. A profound sense of pressure still weighed heavily on him, amplifying the tension of his hidden life. He felt he could explode at any moment, like one of Tee's Mountain Dew cans in the ice box.

The danger of discovery loomed closer than ever, complicating the secrecy of his mission alongside the genuine friendships he'd cultivated. With a growing sense of unease, he turned back toward the garage, a wave of nausea washing over him as he felt a drain of his life force. Tee and Bee had become more than mere acquaintances; they had become his lifeline to a world he had grown to love. He felt an intense responsibility to shield them from Karl, as he would never forgive himself if something happened to either of them on his watch.

"That was a really brave thing you did back there for me with the hockey stick, Tee," Nick admitted to him.

"Thanks. Well, it's technically my garage. Or it will be soon. I might as well learn to defend it now, especially for friends."

"You're a brave young man. I'm glad you're safe. If he had charged at you, I would have reverted to my extraterrestrial form and come to your aid."

"Even if Bee saw?"

"Well, yes, even if Bee saw. And I'll leave the garage in better shape for you than I found it, mate."

"You already have."

Tee inquired about the other modifications or repairs Nick had been adding to his list for the car. Nick rattled off both mid-sized and more minor repairs and projects, including the cowling cover for the windshield, which was brittle and cracked; the Numeric Racing adjustable short throw shifter swap, along with the shift knob replacement; the polished aluminum dash cluster trim; the colored seat belt re-web and swap; the aluminum racing steering wheel; and several plastic cap nuts he described as twisting to secure various housings, weather strips, and a rubber plug that was missing from the front storage to keep moisture from the locking headlight mechanism.

"We'll also be swapping the wheels to new, custom machined aerospace-grade, lightweight, 6061-T6, forged and diamond-cut, aluminum alloy replacements, which are seventeen inches in diameter and will be suitable for the track, mate."

Tee looked around as if he were seeking a pencil to take notes or looking for Acme AI as if she were possibly rattling off the descriptions instead of Nick.

Nick continued, "But the very next task will be the rotors and pads."

"Brake pads?" The boy inquired.

"Yeah, that's right." Nick made a sound to clear his throat. "But let's go for a drive now, and we'll start on that tomorrow."

"And the air intake!" Tee added, with a hint of motivation.

"Oh, yeah, that too." Nick handed Tee the key to the Porsche.

It was a beautiful afternoon. The dust devils must have triggered the puffy cumulus cotton clouds overhead, which then reflected streams of violet and tangerine ribbons from the fading desert sky. It was a classic scene from a postcard but where moisture still lingered in the air and where the picture lacked the smooth lines and reflection of a perfect sportscar, still hidden in a desert garage.

"I think you're ready," Nick remarked, motioning his human head atEe to slide into the driver's seat. Nick unlatched the garage bay door nearest to the car, and Tee settled in as the sound of the rolling steel door coiled overhead.

Nick then settled into the car, closing the passenger side door, his voice calm and reassuring. "Alright, first things first. The clutch is all about feel. You'll want to press it all the way down before you even think about shifting. Got it?"

Tee nodded, swallowing his nerves. He glanced at the gear stick, nesting his hands here and there until each found a grip where they wanted to settle. He was well-versed in changing gears on his dirt bike; the concept was familiar. "Press down, then shift. I got it," his confident voice said.

Nick chuckled, his tone light. "Yeah, you've got it. It's all about listening to the car, feeling its rhythm. Every vehicle speaks to its driver if you know how to listen. Now, since I've backed it in, just go right into first gear, and we'll pull out slowly."

Nick imagined Tee in the garage with his late father. The smell of gasoline and the sound of tools clanking against concrete had most likely been his childhood soundtrack. His father had shown him how machines worked—the intricate dance of pistons and gears, the joy of fixing something with your own hands. It was a bond that had defined their relationship. It was Tee's safe haven he now sought to overtake.

Tee twisted the key, and the engine roared to life, then adapted into a rich and lively purr. As he adjusted the rearview mirror, his reflection met Nick's encouraging human eyes. Slowly, he pressed the clutch, shifted the gear stick into first, and felt the car respond beneath him.

"Easy does it," Nick murmured. "Let's take her out for a spin." The car slid forward with ease, the engine's purr a symphony of precision.

Tee drove out of the garage and onto the winding desert path that stretched up and out of the shallow canyon, then onto the pavement. The wind curled by the open windows, delivering them the scent of sunbaked asphalt mixed with the warm moisture closing in from the clouds. They exchanged stories about their first driving experiences; Nick shared tales from his past missions on Earth, his tone filled with a nostalgic fervor that deepened Tee's curiosity.

Acme Amy's monotone voice broke in. "Tee, did you know that the Porsche 996 GT2 Clubsport MKII has a 3.6-liter engine capable of producing 483 horsepower? It's quite the machine you're handling."

Tee chuckled, his tension easing. "Thanks, A. Not that I needed any more pressure." He shifted gears. "How is the new air suspension functioning?"

"It has been installed and calibrated perfectly, Tee. Feel free to use the control unit."

Nick leaned back, watching the road. "Not just yet," he replied to both Tee and Acme. "You're doing great, kid. Did I ever tell you about Ferdinand Porsche and the history of his sportscar?"

"I can tell you that too." Acme Amy continued.

"Ehe, well, maybe I want to!" Nick yelled back, stopping her.

As they cruised down the desolate road, Nick recounted the tale. "Ferdinand Porsche was an engineering genius. Ehe, he created the first electric hybrid car, actually. He also submitted plans to Volkswagenwerk, or the 'Volkswagen car company.' His designs and concept were chosen over other engineers, and that's how the VW Beetle came into existence. He also designed the Mercedes-Benz SS, which was a famous racer in the 1920s. His son Ferry Porsche joined the company and developed the first Porsche car with his father."

"How do you know all of this?"

"I love cars, mate. The original Porsche 356 was crafted using numerous components from the Volkswagen Beetle. Ferdinand Porsche, who designed both vehicles, strategically incorporated readily available Volkswagen parts to reduce production costs while achieving a distinctive sports car aesthetic with the 356 model."

"What parts did he use?" Tee asked.

"The engine block, suspension parts, and some other chassis components."

Nick then explained how he seized an original Porsche 356 years ago and transported it to Vetu, where he performed a full EV and hover conversion on the Aquamarin Blue Speedster. Tee said he wanted to see it, prompting Nick to display an image from his mobile of the 356 captured with him, alongside two otherworldly beings.

"Wow! There're no wheels? Who are the other two people?" Tee glanced over as he shifted the car's gear stick.

"That's my pop. No wheels, mate."

"Who's the other person he looks younger?" Tee pressed.

Nick, paused for a few beats until things got strangely quiet. "Karl," he muttered.

"Whaaaat?" Tee carried out a surprised and curious tone.

"I'll tell you later." Nick interrupted before Tee could ask anything else. "Keep your eyes on the road, mate," Nick continued unenthusiastically.

Tee dampened his excitement but chimed in with another question as if to maintain their prior sentiment. "Who designed the 911?"

"Ferry Porsche and his son, Ferdinand II, AKA 'Butzi' Porsche. In all the following models, its original iconic fastback styling has shone through, which Butzi insisted upon. A consistent thread over the years."

"A real family business, I guess. So, Karl knows all this stuff too?"

Nick's expression darkened. "Karl has always been well-informed, perhaps too well. He's known about Porsche's lineage and history for a long time. It's part of how he stays ahead—an obsession with detail and knowledge. Actually, he may not remember as much as I do now that he's gone mad."

With every twist and turn on the road, Tee's confidence grew, the initial hesitance fading into assuredness. The car responded to his touch as if acknowledging his presence as he downshifted on turns and upshifted on straightaways. As they looped back toward the garage, the smells of the desert and the sounds of rustling palms united with the rhythmic tune of the GT2 returning home.

"Nice and easy, bring her in," Nick instructed, observing Tee's precise maneuvering as he navigated the Porsche back into the dim garage. The scent of engine oil returned, grounding them in the reality of a bit more hard work yet to be done.

Parking the car, Tee turned off the ignition and exhaled a long, happy breath. He glanced at Nick, who gave a nod of approval. "You've got the touch. You've got it now," Nick said. "Trust yourself, and you'll do fine. We've got more work ahead, but this? You've got it now!"

Tee beamed. Nick could see the warmth of accomplishment spreading through him. "Yeah, it's just like riding a bike," he commented. Nick looked puzzled. Tee laughed, "A motorcycle!" he followed.

"Well, yes and no," Nick remarked.

"Can I sleep in the ETV tonight?" Tee firmly asserted that he'd already informed his mother of his plans to be at the garage that evening with a friend. The boy's eager expression proved too earnest to dismiss.

"I suppose," Nick conceded, "but don't touch anything."

The following day, Nick and Tee focused on the new task, gathering tools and parts necessary for the brake and rotor swap. The sounds of metal clanking and tools scraping echoed within the dilapidated walls again, the mechanical resurrection still mounting.

"We can't afford to waste any more time. We need this car to be perfect." Nick realized that swapping all four rotors and brake pads was a demanding task requiring at very least the remainder of the day to ensure it was completed with proper cleaning, greasing, and torque specifications.

Nick surveyed the various components laid out on the workbench, his extra-long green fingers smoothly coaxing each piece with practiced precision. Tee's wide eyes stared beside him with a mixture of anticipation and excitement.

"Braking performance is critical in racing," Nick explained, his voice steady and authoritative. "It's not just about speed, it's about control. Knowing when to brake can be the difference between victory and disaster. When you're on the track, brake pads heat up quickly," Nick continued, wiping sweat and grime from his head. "You need materials that can withstand high temperatures without losing grip. That's why we chose these—PFC Racing brake pads." He stepped closer to the workbench as Tee continued to listen. "The car was originally sold with Brembos, which is the best brand. That's OEM. But for the racing Cup Series, Porsche uses PFC with a 62-millimeter pad sweep. They're known for high-performance braking technology, made in the United States. They're known globally, and they've forged a strong partnership with Porsche. Two compounds are specifically designed for the 996 model. The 11 compound for sprint racing and the 8 compound for endurance racing. They have a slight friction rise with temperature and a smooth bite, mate."

Tee held the pads, inspecting them as he turned them over to Nick. "Why doesn't Porsche sell them on street cars? How much are they?"

"They don't brake well until they're really hot, mate, then they're superior," Nick affirmed, "five hundred and fifteen U.S. dollars for a set—that covers two wheels, mate. It's four pads," Nick chuckled. "Of course, we'll be doing the rear pads as well."

They soon began replacing the pads. The sentiment felt almost tangible as if the spirit of the renewed garage itself was fully alive with camaraderie.

Nick took a moment to delve deeper into racing principles, offering Tee insights he'd gleaned over centuries of experience.

"Stability is just as important as speed," Nick pointed out, tightening a bolt. "When cornering at high speeds, the suspension keeps the car grounded. Maintains balance. Without it, you'd lose control and spin out—especially with this car, it's only rear wheel drive, as you know. But it's a powerful puppy."

He watched as Tee's hands stilled for a moment, more questions hidden behind his eyes. Nick felt a pang of empathy. Tee reminded him of himself before the weight of intergalactic expectations and the secluded life on Vetu etched lines of cynicism into his psyche. Tee's earnest desire to learn stirred something buried deeply within Nick—a hope that had dimmed but never truly extinguished.

"Nick," Tee asked hesitantly, "Do you think I'll ever be able to race like you?"

Nick paused, turning to meet Tee's gaze. "You've got the passion, Tee. You'll get there if it's what you want to do."

After a long day of mechanics, the remainder of the afternoon slipped away. The wind had blown the sun quickly near the horizon, darkening the lively whistling windows.

"I've got a tennis match with Bee later tonight," he said casually, wiping his hands on a rag.

Tee looked up, intrigued. "I'll sleep in the ETV tonight if that's all right."

Nick chuckled, nodding his head. "Just don't touch—" he stopped himself. "Okay, you've got it, young man."

Nick drove the Porsche to the city again but in his human form, with the sparkling tennis racquet resting in the passenger seat. The night sky was filled with scattered clouds, but the upcoming lesson promised to be lively and filled with playful challenges. It was a warm night, and Bee stood waiting in the parking lot with her summer tennis outfit and radiant smile illuminated by the court lights.

Their laughter mingled with competitive spirit as they stroked balls beneath the clouds, creating a comforting atmosphere that eased Nick. Bee's form was effortless and graceful. Nick steadily maintained his footwork while fully immersed in the thrill of each moment but held onto his confidence tightly from the pleasure of her delightful captivation.

Bee's laughter was like a cozy blanket. She showed every sign of adoring Nick and playfully swatted him with her racquet again, encouraging him to practice. The full white moon eventually hung through the clouds as the night cleared, casting crystal light over their faces. Their shared laughter resonated into the night, and Nick felt a gentle peace within himself.

After a few lessons, a few rallies, and a few games, they agreed to extend their evening by indulging in a frozen yogurt treat, a surprisingly new experience for Nick. As they strolled along the sidewalks together, Nick playfully insisted that it was still ice cream at heart. As Bee argued the concept, Nick finally yielded, and their laughter filled the air, melting away any suspicion she had carried from his unbelief.

They both cherished the moments spent in the present, sharing the gift of life together. Nick held his emotions at bay in the warmth of their friendship, fully aware of the trials awaiting him in the coming days. He enjoyed his time as if each moment was their last.

Returning to the garage, Nick felt an unfamiliar warmth blossoming in his chest. Tee's earnest questions, Bee's spreading energy—it was all starting to chip away at his fortress of solitude. The persistent uncertainty about the future began to claw deeper at him. During their tennis games, Bee inquired again whether he would attend her upcoming tennis tournament, a proposal he felt compelled to accept.

He desperately hoped he could postpone his departure to Vetu until after her final match, as he needed ample time for travel delays. Complex feelings inside him culminated, but for the remainder of the evening, he blocked them and allowed his sense of belonging to hold strong.

The next morning, Nick glided again towards the city along Rose Ruby Parkway in the GT2, but past the tennis courts, this time with Bee in the Porsche while Tee followed in her Honda. "It's an hour's drive to Xpel customs," Nick remarked, stealing a glance at Bee. Her honeysuckle flavor permeated the car's interior, filling Nick's face and mind with pipe dreams of a new future.

"We'll get there in forty minutes with this car!" Bee responded playfully. Their bond flourished effortlessly. The diamond earrings were pinned in her ears, their brilliance reflecting a sea of seven colors.

As they pressed toward the city, they engaged in lighthearted conversation about Bee's ambitions and plans for her tennis career. Nick praised her relentless determination and work ethic.

"You know, your knowledge of cars is quite impressive, too," Bee replied appreciatively and somewhat embarrassed, deflecting Nick's compliments. She began to open up, to share how she was juggling her busy schedule, balancing tennis and work with little or no time to spare.

"That's a good thing, right?" Nick assumed, offering another compliment, but Bee's mood shifted. She confessed that being too occupied felt like a disadvantage—after all, she was still single.

"I just don't have time for a relationship," her voice was laced with a hint of frustration.

Nick reassured her that focusing on her career was perfectly acceptable. "Well, you can do both at the same time! You can make some time to find someone while you establish your path." He was confident in her.

Bee pondered aloud the unpredictability of romance, wondering if perhaps she might miss out on meeting her soulmate altogether while prioritizing her professional aspirations. It was a classic human conflict, career versus family. She elaborated as if to telegraph her feelings for him as if she was trying to reach him. He felt as though she was on the verge of giving voice to the powerful, unspoken pull that seemed to draw them together.

Pausing, Nick glanced over and eased her concerns. "Well, you have two eyes, so keep one eye on the ball and the other on your man, mate!" he laughed, and so did she. He wished it could be him.

Bee turned quiet, then pulled out a small plastic baggie from her purse and held it up to her chin for display, "I brought blueberries if you get hungry."

She had a way of winning him over. He genuinely thanked her for her thoughtfulness and then questioned her music favorites. He began scrolling the satellite radio, searching for lively tunes. Her tone became playful as she pulled on the glovebox lever again. She laughed when her fingers gave up on the locked handle. "Oh, I love this song!" she rasped with excitement. The smooth sounds of Lionel Richie filled the car. "Stuck On You" reverberated through the speakers.

"You know, I love Motown!" he exclaimed over the music. Their voices merged in joyful harmony as they both sang a few lines together.

"Guess I'm On-n-n my way-y-y..." they sang from their bellies and from their hearts, as their eyes locked.

Bee freed her ponytail, and the wind rushed along the lowered windows, tousling her creamy blond hair. Then she couldn't resist a cheeky remark. "Hey, slow down a bit! You're losing Tee behind us."

Nick flashed a furrow of his brow and peered into the rearview mirror, spotting Tee in her silver Honda. "I love that shade of silver. It's like aluminum. I have a craft in that color," he remarked. With his joyful sentiment, he wasn't careful with his words. "Ehe, s-silver matches your style," he covered up.

"Oh, you have a boat?" she inquired.

"Oh, I mean, I did." He slammed the gas pedal abruptly to increase their speed and contradict her playfully. "This boy better keep up!" he shouted but then eased off the gas quickly. Bee burst into laughter she couldn't hold back.

The three of them gallivanted around town, worry-free, creating a day that filled Nick with a sense of shared camaraderie, excitement, and friendly affection. They ran Nick's errands for the day with cherished laughs he felt they'd all surly remember until the end of time.

Several more days came to pass. Nick, Tee, Bee, and the 996 performed their dance of life as the universe intended, somehow intertwining their lives through the cosmos. Things progressed for all three of them, and with the cherished Porsche, enough to satisfy Nick for a time, who eventually entertained brief breaks in his daily routines.

Bee and Tee each accompanied him to the Porsche dealership on various occasions, engaging with Kiev and Dave to acquire essential components for the racer. On some of their adventures, the three drove Bee's car to the city. When only a pair of them were together, they drove the 996.

At one point, Nick paused the racer project altogether, dedicating time to revitalizing the ghost town garage and pruning the three wise men with Tee. It provided Nick with a sense of pleasure and new emotions. He felt the warmth of his friends defragment him somehow and revitalize his nature.

He replaced the gashed windows but sustained several that were merely cracked, explaining to Tee that they added charm to the shop.

His world had finally calmed in general, heralded by the soft sound of birds announcing early spring and desert critters burrowing in the rooted brush, the slight rustle of fanned palm leaves swaying in the gentle breeze, and the occasional thud of a coconut dropping onto the sand.

As the Easter holiday came to pass, the racing project was on the brink of completion. Nick had finished all the major Porsche upgrades he wished to manage independently, save for the K&N Performance air intake modification. Next, he would dispatch the vehicle to RS Customs for the final touch.

Tee enjoyed his restful spring break from school while sharing Nick's continued excitement in the 996. He prepared for the adventure ahead by packing a bag with extra belongings to carry on his dirt bike.

He explained to Nick how he'd notified his mother about staying at the shop, like the many weekends he'd spent there with his father. He also reminded Nick of his upcoming birthday. He mentioned that after taking full ownership of the garage, he would launch a business dedicated to overhauling and modifying dirt bikes, thanks to Nick's inspiration.

Nick relaxed upstairs in the loft, reading a paperback in a comfortable chair near the rail overlooking the shop. The sound of metal echoed through the garage while Tee wrestled with the last of the minor Porsche replacements, his hands slick with sweat and his muscles tensed in concentration.

Tee had devoted the past hour to replacing the air intake but abandoned that pursuit to detach the old, blown-out shock absorber for the decklid secured by the original hooks. He was attempting to swap it with the genuine Porsche replacement, featuring a restored load support and updated clip designs. Beads of sweat formed on his forehead, reflecting the dim rope of bulbs dangling overhead. Each creak and groan of the parts seemed to mock his every move.

Tee exhaled sharply, dropping a tool onto the floor with a metallic clatter. He stepped back, wiped his forehead with the back of his hand, and furrowed his brows into deep lines of aggravation.

Nick's thoughts drifted back to his own struggles when he first vacationed on Earth. The planet's sheer variance in technology had overwhelmed him. He had felt woefully inadequate. His green skin tingled with the memory of those early days; even turning a doorknob was foreign to him. He'd been filled with self-doubt and uncertainty. Recollections of feeling lost surfaced, intertwining with Tee's struggle, serving as a hard-formed reminder of his own journey. It wasn't easy to mentor someone, especially when their enthusiasm was tempered by inexperience.

Tee took a deep breath and slumped onto an old crate, his eyes scanning the garage walls filled with tools, sketches, and remnants of past projects. As Nick watched him over the rail from the corner of his eye, he could see a history of trials and errors, triumphs and losses. Tee slouched quietly as if to contemplate the hours of camaraderie and the growing desire to make something of himself.

Nick stepped down the stairs with a calm demeanor, breaking the silence. "You're doing well, Tee. Take a break.

How about those Mountain Dews?" His voice carried a blend of empathy and authority.

Tee looked up, meeting Nick's eyes. "It's just... I can't seem to fit it right. It doesn't work at any angle." He walked to his bike to retrieve the soda pops from his lunch satchel.

"Maybe if you'd tie your shoe?" Nick watched Tee's dragging shoelace. "Are they still cold?" Nick asked as Tee grabbed the cans from the white pouch. "Why didn't you put them in the icebox?" he inquired, as the boy had frequently accessed the shop's beat-up refrigerator for some time during his visits.

"I just put ice in the bag," he said. The kid had been too lazy to walk upstairs.

"Nothing like a good 'ol pod shrinker to wet the 'ol kisser," Nick started his banter. Tee laughed, then they popped their tops and quenched their thirst together.

Tee's frustration eventually melted away, and he resumed his project. With each correct adjustment, the shock clips—an easy job now—began to respond, lifting and settling in place.

Nick nodded with a proud grin. "You did it, Tee. Just remember to take a break once in a while," he chuckled.

"Thanks, Nick. Yeah, it's easy once you understand the engineering. It's actually easier to work on than most things I've handled. It's just a bit different to learn."

Nick's determination mounted. "Let's finish the air intake," he said, clearing his throat and pulling over the rolling caster workbench. "We need this car to be perfect."

Tee handed Nick a wrench, and they finished tightening and adjusting the modification as needed. Tee's voice broke through Nick's reverie. "Nick, do you think we can really beat Karl? I mean, he's got the 997."

"We'll outsmart him. We have a lighter car and a tuned engine, now with equal horsepower or even more than his. Our modifications are pushing around 550 horses. Plus, we've got something Karl doesn't have."

"What's that?"

"The Acme AI!" he reminded Tee, still doubting its reliability. He thought about selling himself more deeply as he voiced the idea to Tee and tried to curb the boy's uncertainty.

"561 horsepower," Acme AI announced.

Tee nodded, and with his hands steady, he resumed working alongside Nick.

Karl's confusion about the whereabouts of the Acme technology strengthened Nick's confidence. He felt hopeful that even if he didn't win the race, he still had a chance to beat Karl.

Each component they installed and adjustment they made carried the weight of his hopes and fears. But working kept his anxiety at bay. Amidst all their clinks and hums, Nick found a refuge of solace—a place where dreams could be forged in the heat of shared passion and sweat.

Finally, with their shop tasks complete, Nick turned to Tee. "We'll be ready. Karl won't know what hit him." The confidence in his voice was unwavering—a vibration of assurance that promised victory and vindication.

As night began to creep across the desert, ending the day, the two stood back, admiring their work. The bodywork remained, but for now, they'd finished.

As they rested and conversed about technology, shared funny stories, and dreamed of the garage's future, a new vehicle began to approach. Tee moved to the cracked window, and Nick casually told him it was pizza time. He then inquired if Tee liked pizza, which Tee, not to his surprise, confirmed. The pizza driver rolled to a stop on the gravel with two large, steaming pizzas adorned with an array of toppings that Nick had selected on his phone.

Nick avoided revealing himself by directing Tee to handle the exchange with the driver, saving him the toll on his alien body from mutating again. Instead, he walked out back and tightened the flapping blue solar tarp.

Then the two of them enjoyed their pie and dosed up on the two-liter bottle of Mountain Dew that Nick ordered along with the pizzas. They continued leisurely chatting about the exciting upcoming plans.

"Get some rest, Tee. We've got a long weekend." He spoke of their journey to RS Customs in Vegas, where they would finalize details with the owner and leave the Porsche for a full two weeks of modifications. "Then, when it's finished, we need to test its limits. So, while we're waiting, we'll build a track out back," Nick gathered his thoughts aloud, directing his eyes toward the back of the garage as if he were seeing through its walls, imagining a completed makeshift track.

Tee nodded, a smile crossing his face. "I'll sleep in the ETV tonight if that's all right."

Nick took some extra time that night to sit in the Porsche's driver's seat. He gripped the steering wheel, closing his eyes to imagine the roar of the engine, the thrill of acceleration, and the seamless glide around the track. He transported his mind back to the burning excitement of racing, the cheer of the crowd ringing in his ears like an old, reverent song.

A sense of peace comforted him, but a pang of sadness accompanied it. Bee and Tee's warmth had become an anchor to his life on Earth. The race was approaching, and he couldn't help but feel the shadow of his departure encroaching over the fragile connections.

Nick's thoughts turned inward, reflecting on the countless hours spent with Tee, laboring over the car. Laughter had filled the garage during moments of victory, whether fitting the new brake pads or marveling at the precision of a perfect tuning. Frustration, too, had played its part, teaching patience through aggravated bolts and stubborn components. Or, worse, the day Tee discovered Nick's identity. Tee's enthusiasm and eagerness to learn were those of a pure soul with intention. And Bee, he couldn't even think about Bee right now; it was too heavy for his heart.

He pondered the broader implications of his journey, which began many years ago with his visits to Earth solely to watch the cars race at Le Mans. Memories of the bright racers darting by, the camaraderie in the pits, and the excited murmurs of spectators mingled with his present reality.

On Vetu, he was but a solitary figure, an Old Dog, wading through the tide of an advanced world of technology and calculated exchanges. He feared the cold distance of Vetu, where interactions felt more transactional, devoid of the warmth he found on Earth. Friendships like those with Tee and Bee weren't easily formed or forgotten. Here, on Earth, he'd found something he hadn't realized he was missing. It was the earnest connection between hearts bound by shared feelings and passions.

However, he thought of his impending return to Vetu and how it also brought notes of excitement. The upcoming race and car show promised all the glory, a chance to reclaim his standing and finally prove his worth. But, the thought of severing ties with the human friends he had grown to cherish left an ache in his heart.

Nick quietly stepped outside the shop to ponder, feeling the cool desert breeze against his alien skin. The wind had blown the clouds to the west, and the stars shimmering above possessed a brilliance. He gazed up, his mind a whirlwind of thoughts and reflections. This mission on Earth, which started as a quest for a classic, had become much more complicated and meaningful. The vastness of the universe above exposed the reality of the distance between his two lives.

He leaned over to toss his paper cup into the oversized steel drum, which rested beside the other toppled drum clumsy Karl had infringed on weeks ago. Among the trash inside, he spotted Tee's vape pen. The kid had thrown it away.

He took a deep breath and exhaled slowly. As their bond had deepened, the notion of leaving Tee gnawed at his bones. Nick's profound compassion for how the boy had lost his father consumed him. He didn't want to leave the boy alone.

His determination, bright curiosity, bravery, and the fight for life inside him were pure.

And Bee—her infectious laughter, her unwavering kindness—had opened a door to a part of himself he had long buried, one that yearned for deserved connection and companionship.

Nick resolved to cherish the time he had left and make the most of his life on Earth before fate drew him back home. The connections he found had changed him, bridging a gap between worlds within his heart. Even as the thrill of the upcoming race beckoned, he understood these moments of laughter, shared struggles, and intermittent joys were just as significant—if not more.

Whatever the future held, he would carry these experiences with him—testaments to the depth of human connection and shared dreams that transcended the boundaries of a universe.

Chapter Nine

The three of them arrived in the city at RS Customs to connect with Rod, the shop owner, and finalize the arrangements. Nick and Bee drove the 996 while Tee followed in Bee's Honda again.

Rod, a young Chinese enthusiast, also owned a Porsche 911. He confidently assured Nick of a "special deal," sharing his passion for the icon. Upon arrival, Nick saw his striking pink 992—the eighth-generation Carrera—parked out front, showcasing Porsche's latest vibrant color—Ruby Star Nio.

However, Nick's gaze was then drawn through the fiery sun to the bay door, where a stunning Indian-red Porsche 997 Turbo serendipitously rested inside. The provocative aerodynamic surface blinged under the shop's LEDs. The dark resin carbon fiber rear spoiler hinted at the raw power that lay within. 88-millimeters wider in the rear than Nick's car, its aggressive stance, complemented by the striking red hue, radiated a sense of urgency and passion, leaving a lasting impression on those fortunate enough to lay eyes on it.

Nick squinted away from the searing desert sun, feeling the heat radiate from the blacktop as he and Tee eagerly approached the 997, Bee trailing behind. Tee's eager young heart remained quiet despite knowing who the Porsche owner was, keenly examining the car's exterior as if etching it into memory. The windows were down, releasing a faint lingering scent of stale smoke as they walked around the car. They noticed a fat, golden-labeled Black Box cigar stub resting charred in the console.

Tee suggested to Nick that they ask Rod to pop the deck lid of the 997 under the pretense of admiring the vehicle, but Nick refused to entertain the idea and stood back. He didn't care about the tuning of Karl's Porsche. He cared about his own.

Bee admired the red racer and asked Nick several questions, occasionally prompting Tee to pipe up with answers. As she circled the vehicle, her interest suddenly waned, leading her to address Nick. "I feel nauseous. We should go. I need something to settle my stomach." She held her hand over her belly.

Nick, puzzled, inquired about her drastic change in demeanor. She replied, "The sight of the cigar upset my stomach."

"The sight?" he echoed.

"The smell. I didn't eat anything today. Let's leave, please?" she urged earnestly, and they promptly pivoted.

Nick pressed Rod to prioritize protecting his car, insisting that no bystanders examine his 996. He detailed the significance of an important upcoming car show out of town.

The idea of sending his Porsche to a different shop strongly crossed his mind, driven by the desire to protect it from Karl, but it was too late; the race was approaching, so he rolled the dice.

Bee withdrew to the distance as Nick recapped modifications with Rod. Within moments, the three of them set off on their way to care for Bee and explore the vibrant city. Nick softly embraced each precious moment with his dear friends as his cherished time ticked away.

The full two weeks came to pass while the crew remained engaged in various activities. Tee enjoyed quality time with his mother and sister some days, while Nick and Bee participated in racquet activities together, including casual singles and doubles matches in the city, even a round-robin pickleball rally. Nick's alone time without his car prompted calls to his friends on Vetu and walks around the garage every morning to survey the area. He saved breadcrumbs for the roadrunner and marveled at the desert lizards darting about.

On Bee's work days, he rode a bicycle to meet her at Slotsky's for lunch, where they both got to know Darla, and Nick even gambled a few of Bee's dollars in the slot machines. They visited the cinema and practiced holding hands. Bee also reserved time for herself, attending her ITF league tennis matches, grinding her way to the top. Although things moved at a relaxed pace, Bee, at a later point, swiftly planted a delicate kiss on Nick's cheek—a gentle gesture that danced just shy of his lips.

However, RS Customs was lagging behind schedule. Nick's anxiety began to surge as the completion of his Porsche lingered in uncertainty. He masked his unease, striving to maintain a facade of normalcy in his day-to-day life.

That week, he struck the tennis ball with greater intensity to release his frustrations. He also reached out to his friend Azi and other friends more frequently than usual, hoping for reliable counsel or reassurance.

Nick began phoning Rod daily. After a lengthy three-and-a-half weeks, RS Customs had far surpassed the timeline for completing the necessary modifications. Rod appeared to be feeding Nick a comforting narrative instead of revealing the genuine reasons for the delays and a realistic timeline for completing the project.

"Just be square with me, mate, or I'll come pick up the car! I'll pay you your money! Rod! Or whatever your name is!" he felt frustrated and a surge of worry as he imagined Karl probing into Rod's shop, sabotaging his GT2. If needed, Nick would transport the unfinished car to Vetu and enter it into the race as it was. The aesthetics would surely cost him the car show prize but not the race itself, which remained his priority.

Finally, Rod made the call, and Nick, accompanied by his dedicated human friends, retrieved his finished Porsche. Nick, Tee, and Bee were absolutely enthralled when they caught sight of the car.

Its deep black, newly polished surface, coated with an invisible ceramic finish, reflected their faces like an obsidian mirror. The fresh GTS rear bumper, featuring shark gills and intricately meshed air scoops, and wide offset wheels gave the car an intense presence. The golden Porsche crest that Nick replaced on the hood sparkled with brilliance. The 55% tinted windows showcased a subtle blue glare.

The new piano-black gloss interior trim provided a fresh look to the cabin, offering a modern contrast to the old cracked and oxidized carbon fiber pieces. Its dazzling monochrome interior accentuated the new, vibrant racing-red seat belts.

With a generous spirit, Nick handed over the keys, allowing Bee to take the wheel of the striking gem as they sped back to Rose Ruby.

With only three days left to seize the opportunity, it was crucial to push the car to its limits and unleash the true power of the GT2. This last assessment could uncover any issues the car might have before the final day it would need to be loaded in the ETV.

Short on time, Nick felt anxious and apprehensive. However, Tee remained eager, an energy that had pulled Nick through more than a few tiring days. He was unsure of Nick's departure date since Nick rarely discussed it, usually just telling Tee the time would come after the car was complete.

"Ready for this, N?" Tee teased with a nickname, a smirk curling his lips as he palmed the Porsche key, ready to drive it himself. Nick accepted with a playful grunt.

"Let's see if your tinkering holds up," Nick replied, snatching the key from him and sliding into the driver's seat.

"Let's do it!" Tee coiled up the steel bay door while Bee stepped back and watched.

"Let's keep the windows rolled up, though, to keep the dust out. And we'll wash it after," Nick added.

The interior of the Porsche was filled with a new sense of pleasure. Nick placed his hands on the custom wheel, the cool aluminum conforming to his grip. The engine roared to life, vibrating through his bones with a deep, primal growl—a tune that explained why he loved machines; the blend of power and precision.

With Tee in the passenger seat, offering pointers and encouragement, Nick carefully navigated the dirt track they'd formed outside the garage.

Bee found a seat on the steel drum near the garage entrance to observe the test run. Nick had opted to finally build the track in front of the garage on the opposite side, far from the concealed ETV, for that very reason.

He was weary from sending Bee away so many times and crafting excuses to shield his secretive life. So, he set about modifying his journey to integrate her more fully into his world. If she'd seen the makeshift track extending from behind the garage, she might have inquired, and it wouldn't have been appropriate for Nick to leave her without a tour. Regardless of any lame excuse, he could have urgently contrived.

He pleasantly directed her to keep her eyes on the Porsche as they raced the track, staying alert to assist with any exterior issues that may develop with the car.

The driving was smooth, with the freshly installed air suspension gracefully absorbing bumps and dips. Nick let out a whoop of appreciation, impressed by the racer's noticeable improvement.

"Looks like our adjustments did the trick," Nick called over the engine's rumble after a few roaring rounds of the track.

Tee beamed. "Now, try to hit the brakes."

The car responded flawlessly. Nick slammed the brake pedal, putting the pads into action. The antilock system clattered as needed, and the Porsche came to an abrupt, controlled stop. The tires kissed the tough desert dirt with a perfect bite. He felt a swell of pride in the car's performance and Tee's growing confidence.

After the dust settled, they switched seats on Nick's recommendation. He watched the boy with a mixture of envy and admiration. His youthful eagerness reminded Nick of the good 'ol days. The boy had his whole life in front of him.

Tee took the wheel with natural ease. Under Nick's watchful eye and intermittent guidance, the boy pushed the Porsche through its gears, gliding over the dirt with assurance. With every wheel twist and press of the pedal, he seemed to breathe life into the car with his enthusiasm and smooth shifting.

When they hit the track straightaway, the Porsche's engine roared like a starving bear, vibrating as Tee pushed the tachometer to seven thousand RPMs. Nick saw the boy's grin widen, the thrill of power lighting his eyes.

"Don't push it too hard," Nick warned, though the thrill in his voice suggested that he was just as eager.

Tee nodded, barely able to contain his excitement. "I've got it!" The car slung effortlessly around the bends, hugging the desert track like magic. Nick's chest swelled with pride as he watched Tee grow into a competent driver.

Suddenly, mid-corner, the Porsche shuddered violently and coasted. Tee's face fell. "What just happened?" His eyes darted to Nick as their hearts sank.

Nick's intuition pinpointed the issue almost immediately. "It's the transaxle. It feels like something fell." The two of them hopped out. Nick's heart sank as he spotted the bolt and transaxle dangling precariously, the thread bungled, and the entrance blown.

Acme AI announced, "Screw thread entrance point to transaxle stripped."

"Well, why didn't you catch it earlier when it was loose?" Nick snapped and grunted at the Acme unit, now tempted to rip her out of the car completely.

"It happened quickly, sir," she said robotically without remorse.

The car was caught in limbo and unable to shift into gear. They pushed the 996 as Bee sat behind the wheel, steering toward the garage while parts were hanging and dragging in the dirt.

Tee's face tightened with frustration and sadness. Nick placed a comforting hand on his shoulder. "Well, I'm glad it happened now rather than on race day." He remained calm but mentally tried to assess a timeline for the repair on the brink of his own panic. He roamed the landscape of his thoughts, grappling with the bleak reality of his situation.

He remembered the countless setbacks he'd faced on Vetu, the races he lost due to mechanical failures, and the subsequent hours spent in the workshop. Every breakdown was a lesson, a test of perseverance. The ticking clock filled him with worry, as he feared he might miss the race entirely and wondered if he would ever have the opportunity to restore his reputation.

Nick took a deep breath, allowing the desert air to fill his lungs. He glanced at Tee, who began rolling over the blue workbench with intensity and determination.

Now was not the time to wallow. They had work to do. Nick knew the true measure of a racer wasn't just how fast they went but how they learned to pivot during the journey, both on and off the track—as he'd always said. The path ahead was daunting, but if the journey proved successful, it would be worth every turn, repair, and shared moment of triumph.

Nick surveyed the garage. Scratched and dented tools and parts laid across battered work areas, mingling with the scent of oil and metal shavings from his progress over the past six months. Each piece told a story of his efforts and dreams, the air heavy with anticipation and resolve.

"For this final push, we'll need to reshape the hole for the transmission bolt," Nick planned, his voice steady despite the darkening disaster. "The welder and tapping set should be over there." He nodded in its direction while his hands busied with other things.

"Can't we just order a new mount?" Tee asked.

"It's not the mount. It's the bolt, and this is an old car, so delivery of parts takes time." It was Friday afternoon. "The

Porsche dealership has closed up shop, and we'd be sitting all weekend."

Tee broke into action. "Got it!" he replied, sprinting to retrieve the tools.

Nick began explaining, his fingers tracing the outline of the damaged mount hole. "We'll fill this portion with a torch and welding stick. Then, we'll re-tap it using the tapping set and secure a new bolt with thread locker to ensure it doesn't pull loose again."

As they worked to free the dangling parts, the show of mechanic's grease, smudged their tools, clothes, green skin, and their faces.

The torch's flame rocketed like a serrated edge, melding the metal seamlessly. Nick guided himself through the meticulous process.

"You're sure about this, right?" Tee asked mid-stroke, wiping his hands on his jeans. Nick took a break and lifted his welding mask, which pinched around his large face.

"I've been doing this since you were in diapers," Nick commented, trying to ease the boy's nerves. "Well, about two hundred years before you were born, actually," he trailed off. He could see the unspoken respect deepen in Tee.

He continued to channel his emotions, with tunnel vision, into performing the adequate repair. The stakes of the race were too monumental for Nick's reputation.

"Trust me, kid. We've taken every measure, every modification. Karl's 997 doesn't stand a chance once we're through. He could upgrade as many parts as he wants, and I'll still beat'em! When the penny drops, he'll give me the point-by."

With the final stroke of the torch completed and the tapping process underway, Tee's grimy palm held the large mounting bolt.

"Take a step back and look at it," Nick suggested, wiping his hands on an oil-stained rag. "We've done something incredible here. Only option now."

"What about this, though?" Tee held the stripped bolt with butchered threads.

"Well, we'll need to go to the hardware store, mate."

"How are we going to go without a car?"

"Well..." Nick scratched his cheek. Bee was already gone. He hadn't thought of that. "I'll send you on your motorbike..." He paused. "You put the old bolt in your pocket, ride to the store, and find the new bolt. It's M14 by 1.5. You can text me when you get there if needed."

"What if they don't have it?"

Nick paused. "Then we'll go to another store, mate."

"The other stores are far away in the city. I mean, it would take like two hours on my dirt bike. Plus, it's not street-legal. I guess... I could go home and take my mom's car to the city." He pondered.

"I have an idea." Nick stood at the wide shop sink, diligently lathering his hands with soap from a girthy orange dispenser. "You go to the local store, and I'll order one online from Big Brown." He dried his hands but lifted his phone carefully, thinking about Bee. Tee raced off on the orange tiger as Nick followed through with his last credit card.

As he clicked 'purchase,' Nick's thoughts drifted. He adamantly blocked out visions of missing the race altogether. Instead, he envisioned himself standing proud as the victor, reclaiming his place among those he revered, with the imperial blue ribbon and heavy gold medallion around his neck. He imagined the packed WCACCV2 arena, cheering beyond their means, the faces of competitors and spectators, the echoing chants of names, and the sweet smell and satisfaction of victory.

Nick sat in the loft of the abandoned garage, the old structure creaking slightly in the dust devils from the desert gusts. He swung open the small, square window positioned at the foot of the bed adjacent to a small oak chair and mirrored chest of drawers.

The golden hour cast a warm, almost nostalgic light across the desert landscape, painting the sand and Joshua trees in hues of amber and rose. His eyes fixed on the three wise men and then drifted to the horizon, where the Red Ruby Mountains met the deep blue sky. His mind raced far beyond the stretched horizon. He felt torn between two galaxies.

A slideshow of memories played before him—moments spent with Bee, her laughter echoing in his heart. He recalled their first encounter, her easy smile as they first landed the parcels from her truck together. She had been a burst of starlight in his lonely life. The memory of their tennis matches was as vivid as if it happened yesterday. The feel of the racket in his hands, the thrill of watching her hit a perfect serve, and the shared moments of camaraderie on the silver-lighted clay courts. Bee had a way of making him forget he was an alien, making him feel accepted in the best ways. Gratitude welled up inside him, though tinged with the sharp edge of regret. How deeply he had connected with her, only to face the eventuality of leaving it all behind and breaking her friendly heart.

Nick fetched the tennis racquet by his chest of drawers and gripped it. He couldn't help but replay the scenes of their encounters, from the casual deliveries to the more intimate moments shared over coffee or the tea with her aunt's local honey. Her spark and warmth had unknowingly chipped away at his guarded exterior. Her inquisitiveness, her sheer zeal for life, had been refreshing, continuously drawing him out of his shell. She had changed him forever. Yet he always held back, a half-truth away from complete openness. The weight of his secret was a constant burden, creating a barrier he was both eager and afraid to cross.

His thoughts shifted to the impending race and the starkly different life awaiting him back home. Winning the race had always been the goal, a mission instilled deeply within him. Yet the implications of such a victory now tugged at his heartstrings. He wondered what it would ultimately mean for his budding relationships on Earth.

He closed his eyes, letting the desert winds sift through the window and caress his face. The mixture of gratitude coupled with regret was almost paralyzing. In the stillness, the voices of his fellow racers and friends from Vetu whispered in his mind, urging him to stay focused. The car, his beloved Porsche 996, was more than a mere vehicle. It symbolized his ambition, a tangible link to his past and his dreams for the future. But big dreams, he was beginning to understand, required sacrifice.

Nick could feel a deep longing, an ache that stemmed from knowing he had found something precious and also understanding that he must let it go. Earth had a way of weaving itself into his being, its people and their simple, earnest lives becoming inextricably linked to his journey forever. The Earthlings didn't have the brilliant minds of Vetu, but they had a soulful existence.

Opening his eyes, Nick stared at the barren land once more. The vast emptiness mirrored his sense of isolation. Yet, amidst this, he also saw the beauty and potential for growth. While desolate, the desert was also a place of resilience, much like his journey.

The desert sun faded softly, casting a deep blue, warm, nostalgic haze and orange glow over the prickly sands at nightfall. Nick drew in a deep breath, filling his lungs with the dry, earthy scent of the desert.

He then forced himself away from the window, the worn floorboards groaning under his weight. He couldn't afford to let his feelings cloud his judgment. There was too much at stake now, and every second counted. The task ahead was harrowing, but Nick knew he couldn't let doubt consume him. His mission was clear, even if his heart ached with uncertainty.

With new determination, Nick hardened his spirit and reminded himself of what clearly lay ahead. His mission was an affirmation of his place in the galaxy. Glancing one last time at the fading sunlight, he descended the loft with a determination that tightened his hold on the racquet gripped in hand.

The GT2 sat nearly completed, awaiting one last bolt, full of promise. As he moved with newfound clarity toward the car, Nick knew that every moment spent here would fuel his drives despite the impending farewell. The mission would continue, and though the path was uncertain, his focus was sharpened, ready for the challenges ahead.

Tee returned from the hardware store, his motorcycle stirring up his signature cloud of dust. He proudly pinched from his pocket the perfect bolt for the Porsche. The two secured the transmission with the vital piece, marking a joyous finale to the restoration journey. Nick gently eased the vehicle down from the hydraulic lift. The rack hissed through the garage as they both silently observed the icon slowly descending. It was a finished project, a real racer.

Nick meticulously reviewed his checklist. A looming departure clung to the garage walls while the Porsche beamed under the bowing rope of glass bulbs. Each item on the list bore the weight of countless hours spent stroking the car back to life. From the larger throttle body to the new custom motor mounts, the custom air intake, and so many modifications, a lengthy list, every detail had been fine-tuned.

"Can we go over the rules of the race?" Tee asked, breaking the silence.

"Well, sure. Walk over to that pin board and fetch the list," he directed. Tee pulled the short list of rules from

WCACCV2, copied in Nick's handwriting, and handed it to him. "Number one. Contestants may journey to any time era and any planet in any galaxy, provided that the vehicle they acquire is no less than twenty years old from the moment they arrive on the local planet and justified by the galactic clock." He gave side notes to Tee as he continued, "This refers specifically to the local planet's time but filtered by the multiverse time, mate."

"Ours is Big Ben. I think it's in London," Tee remarked.

"Oh, really? Yes, I think I've heard that before, actually. Interesting." Nick mused.

"Why does Karl have a 2007 model when this year is only 2026? That's only nineteen years," Tee asked and said.

"Well, the 2007 model was released a bit earlier in 2006, mate. But he owns the Turbo 997.1, not the Turbo S model, he claims. The S model was introduced later, in 2010, as the 997.2. Therefore, Karl's Porsche is two decades old but has between seventeen and twenty-seven horsepower less than he claims, before tuning, of course."

"Oh, I see. So, he's a liar."

"That's right. He always was." Nick pressed forward, calling out the rules, "The second rule of the race is that after acquiring your auto, you must safely return it to Vetu. Of course, that's where the race is. The WCACCV2 track.

"Of course."

"Next, should you ever return to the planet from which your classic car originated, you will permanently relinquish ownership of your classic. This regulation is currently in place to ensure the safety of that planet's inhabitants and to prevent any chaos that may arise from the revelation of extraterrestrial existence. While there is a possibility that this rule could be amended in the future, contestants must brace themselves for the certainty that reentry is off-limits. Presently, interplanetary travel is strongly discouraged." Nick trailed off.

Tee paused, then quietly said, "So, you're never coming back."

"Well, I mean, I mean, you know... there are ways to travel, kid. Don't worry. There are excuses sometimes."

Tee slumped quietly on the wooden crate. Nick continued speedily to brighten the sentiment. "Additional modifications will be permitted once your classic car reaches Vetu. So, as long as adequate time remains, scheduled according to galactic time V27:0X, that is, Victor Two Seven Zero X-ray. However, please note that the competition will be an internal combustion street race on solid ground, not an aerial hovercraft or EV race. Here, you read the rest, kid." Nick offered a chance to improve Tee's dispiriting mood.

Tee hunched on the crate, his posture conveying both weariness and contemplation. Nick extended the list to him, its otherworldly crystal-red ink shimmering with a once-vibrant alien glow that had gradually dimmed as months passed.

Tee continued, "After the exhilarating car race, spectators will be treated to an impressive car show, where vehicles are expertly staged for evaluation by judges. Contestants will have the opportunity to meticulously clean their cars in preparation for the evening showcase, so long as the car remains at the event."

"You're a good reader. Okay, there is one more basic rule."

"The vehicle must comply with the regulations for road operation under the jurisdiction of Vetu, and it should bear a likeness to the original model to be evaluated by the panel of judges," Tee concluded. "Cool ink," he remarked. "So, it's gotta be street legal?"

"That's right. You can keep that list. Hold onto it as a keepsake. You helped, whether I win or not." Nick attempted to lift Tee's somber spirits.

"I'll be back tomorrow," Tee finally said, looking at his phone and pocketing the paper. Then regrettably, he left Nick behind and sped away into the darkness on his dirt bike for the family dinner that awaited him.

Once Nick's surroundings silenced, he turned inward to his thoughts and relished the fulfillment of a daunting task now successfully completed.

Early Saturday Morning, Nick rose for a French press and watched the sunrise. He rested in the folding chair outside in front of the shop door as the warm sky awakened into a stunning panoramic of soft pastels. He spotted his roadrunner friend in the distance, with a companion darting next to him, likely a girlfriend. They were both energetically scuttling across the desert spring landscape while Newt grasped a lengthy, fat worm that dangled from his beak. The bird had finally left the garage altogether for spring, no longer returning at night, undoubtedly to nest elsewhere, to hunt and procreate in the warmer weather.

His mind wandered back to the moment he first set foot in the dilapidated shelter. The garage had looked much different then—more a haunted ruin than a workshop. Yet it had become his sanctuary, where he'd forged the interstellar racer. An iconic racing machine that may be the finest in the entire multiverse. Glancing back at the car, he felt another ache in his chest, the rare pang of memories made and bonds formed.

Later that afternoon, Tee came racing back. He was a reliable and faithful boy. As he approached wearing his backpack, he uncovered and cradled a newly minted racing helmet and two Mountain Dews.

"I thought you might need this," Tee said, handing over the glossed black helmet with a sparkling brown stripe. The gesture carried immense weight, serving as a tangible sign of the respect and admiration he held for Nick.

Nick took the helmet, its mirror finish smooth and perfect, just like every detail of the Porsche. Other than the honey from his friend Bee, no person on Earth had ever gifted him anything. He admired it for several moments, then carefully placed it by the stairs to the loft alongside the borrowed tennis racquet leaning against the wall, their weight more than physical.

"Perfect timing," Nick said, trying to mask the lump forming in his throat. "Thanks, Tee."

With a playful nudge, Tee broke the momentary silence. "So, are you ready to smoke Karl's 997?"

"Like a Young Dog, mate," Nick replied with a wink, though the playful banter couldn't entirely mask his underlying dread. His smile didn't last long, returning his blank expression quickly.

Tee's eyes drifted to the garage bay, widening as he noticed the Porsche was gone. "Where's the 996?"

Nick pointed toward the spacecraft. "Loaded and ready."

Tee nodded, a mix of awe and sadness on his face as he took a deep breath, "Good luck out there, Nick." Then Tee strolled out to the ETV while Nick followed.

When they stopped, Nick rested a hand on Tee's shoulder, "It's not just me out there. Everything you've done—it's all part of this. I couldn't have done it without you, Tee."

As they stood together out back, the light of day glared from the freed metallic spacecraft. The scene was both somber and hopeful, a deep remembrance of shared toil and triumphs. Yet, beyond his calm exterior, Nick's heart was a storm of emotions.

He recalled the trials he faced acquiring the Porsche 996, the moment his eyes locked on the run-down garage that symbolized his mission—a mission now regretfully completed. Each interaction with Tee and Bee had taught him about human emotion, resilience, and the unexpected warmth of companionship.

Never had he imagined finding solace in a human partner like Tee, whose youthful exuberance balanced his own cautious pragmatism, making him second-guess the camaraderie he knew back home. With his youthful enthusiasm and thirst for knowledge, Tee had become like a younger brother to him.

Recycling thoughts of Bee brought a different ache—gratitude tinged with regret. Her unwavering support, infectious laughter, and simple companionship were rare treasures throughout the multiverse. He wished he could express just how much her presence had meant to him, yet the truth of his concealed identity had ruined them. He couldn't think of anything meaningful to say to her without risking everything. She didn't deserve to be hurt.

Chapter Ten

The sound of gravel crunching beneath Bee's truck tires snapped him back to reality, and Nick glanced up to see her delivery truck pulling in. Seeing her make her last delivery, blissfully unaware of his turmoil, compounded the emotional discord within him. It was as if the universe mocked him, presenting connections he yearned for but might never be able to sustain.

Bee stepped out of the truck, her ponytail bouncing with each stride. Her smile was like a breath of fresh air, momentarily lifting the weight from his shoulders. As she carried a small package, her face curved into a bright welcome, a smile that made Nick's heart ache with a mixture of joy and sadness.

"Hey, Nick! Got another package for you!"

It was the extra transmission bolt.

Nick forced a smile, trying to match her enthusiasm. "Thanks, Bee. You're the best delivery driver there is, mate." His voice quivered as he took hold of the package, their fingers brushing briefly.

They enjoyed a cup of coffee and chatted about regular things, like the early heat wave that swept the valley and the latest tech in delivery trucks. Nick found solace in the small talk, a temporary distraction from the imminent farewell. Yet there was a tightening knot in his stomach, the foreboding sense, now a conclusion, that this would be their last conversation. He couldn't help but imagine a different future, one where he stayed on Earth and built a life with Bee.

They would spend weekends driving the Porsche and touring the city shows, her laughter filling any place they gathered together, or afternoons playing tennis, feeling the satisfying rubber thud of the yellow ball against the stringed racket. It was presumptuous, but he wondered if such a life was within his grasp or forever out of reach, bound by the rules of his home planet and this contest, or simply the distance of the Milky Way itself.

She then expressed her immense joy about the approaching championship tennis match. With unwavering confidence, she believed that victory was within her grasp, thanks to his helpful encouragement, she explained, a crucial factor in her latest victories on the court. She held two tennis match tickets and explained how Nick's support to attend the championship battle was probably why she knew she would win. It was clear she longed to have him there, so he knew his absence was not an option.

"They're in the box," she stated, handing over the paper tickets. "You can bring Tee too." Her sentiment held a desperate undertone, as if that special day was the heart of everything.

Nick began to respond, "Wha—"

"You get a free hotdog!" She interrupted, then giggled. She had no reason to believe he wouldn't attend the game, but she was worried anyway.

"What's the box?" He jogged his head and smiled to volley back.

"Front row seat... mate." She grinned.

Bee's observant eyes noticed the tension in his posture. She tilted her head slightly to one side, her brows pushing together. "Nick, are you okay? You seem... off."

Nick hesitated, the words caught in his throat. How would he tell her the truth? That he was an alien from another planet, bound by an arbitrary set of rules that dictated he could never return to Earth once he left? He felt the cold grip of his secrets tighten around his heart. "Yeah, just a bit tired. You know how it is, these long hot days."

Bee's face softened with concern. "If you need to talk, you know I'm here, right?"

He wanted to cry out, to tell her everything, to share the weight he was carrying and pull her in his arms. But he knew it wouldn't be fair to her. "Thanks, Bee. I appreciate it."

She looked at him thoughtfully, then glanced at her truck, considering something else. "Should we schedule another tennis match? Maybe this coming weekend?" She sensed his distance. "You'll get to play against the champ!" She smiled and fabricated a chuckle.

The question hung in the air, filled with hope and uncertainty. Nick's body tightened further. He couldn't bring himself to confirm or deny her, fearing that either option would break him. "We'll see," he managed to say, his voice barely above a whisper.

Bee nodded, though the confusion in her eyes was evident. She tucked her lower lip for a second, trying to hide her disappointment. "All right then. Don't be a stranger. I'll text you later?"

"Yeah."

"You look like you need a hug." She stepped in to embrace him, then softly kissed his cheek. "Whatever it is, keep your chin up, mate." She parroted his words but with sincerity.

As she walked away, Nick's heart felt heavier with each of her steps. He watched her elegant silhouette step further from him, outlined by the long desert sunset. The vibrant light she'd brought into his life. He imagined their potential future slipping away like sand through his fingers. The possibilities evaporated with each stride she took away.

"Bee!" he called out.

She turned one last time, offering a smile that carried her warmth. Nick just gleamed at her and, through his eyes, tried to tell her all that he felt.

She was offbeat, but she appeared to stay optimistic. He didn't want to confuse her, but his actions had. As Bee's truck disappeared down the driveway, Nick stood silently, a feeling of forever emptiness closing in on him.

He pondered the fleeting nature of human connections. The bittersweet taste of moments turned into memories. If only he could stay—build on the fragile yet profound bonds he'd formed—but he knew better. He was an interstellar traveler, ultimately bound by different stars and a destiny that would pull him back to his home planet. The ache in his heart whispered of regrets and what-ifs, of roads not taken and words left unsaid.

Nick took a deep breath as he turned back toward the gray garage, which turned pale in the silence of Bee's colorful existence. The new, distinct feeling of her absence felt heavy, each empty space where she once stood holding a fragment of what had been and what could never be. There, with his thoughts and the hum of his burdens, Nick braced himself for the final leg of his journey, knowing that some farewells leave marks that time can neither erase nor mend.

Nick's mind painted vivid images of Tee's eager face as he learned about mounts and bolts, the boy's eyes always bright with curiosity and determination. Tee's enthusiasm had rubbed off on him, reminding Nick of his own glory days in the world of racing. He recalled Tee's strong young hands working on the brake pads, the two of them sharing quiet camaraderie as they turned wrenches side by side. It wasn't just the mechanics but the unspoken bond that had formed, one of mutual respect and understanding. As Nick recounted these memories, he faced the rules of the galactic car contest, which couldn't be broken.

The rivalry with Karl came to the forefront of his mind, his longtime nemesis for years, lurking in the underbelly of the racing world. Karl's presence on Earth had been a thorn in his side, but it also provided a goal—a reason to keep pushing forward. The car show on Vetu wasn't just about bragging rights; it was a chance to reclaim his standing within the World Cars and Coffee Club and, moreover, the entire city, even the whole community around the Creamy Way. If he had to live out the rest of his days on Vetu, then redemption was the finest way to assert his place in the community that had once looked up to him. It was the best his planet had to offer.

His gaze wandered the garage, the shadows from the palm leaves flickering against the walls like scenes from an antique reel. He thought again about what it would mean to remain on Earth, to keep Tee and Bee close. Their friendships had healed parts of him he hadn't realized were broken. He imagined a future where he laughed openly with Bee and continued nurturing Tee's talent, watching the boy grow into the skilled mechanic he was destined to be.

As the white crescent moon grew in the sky, its pale light filtered through the gaps in the garage, Nick felt a soft resolve settle within him. While he couldn't change the rules that bound him, he could honor the memories and the friendships in other ways. He silently vowed to carry them in his heart as he chased victory and faced the unknown. The lessons of friendship, the joy of teaching, and the warmth of being cared for would all stay with him, guiding his path. He would change his life, and he would give back to those around him.

"Nick?" Tee's voice brought him back to the present.

"Sorry, just lost in thought," Nick said, giving Tee a strained smile.

Tee looked at him, his eyes brimming with sincerity. "We've come a long way. No matter what happens out there, we've done well."

Nick nodded, swallowing hard. "Yeah, we did." The words felt weak against the current of emotions threatening to pull him under.

Checking his mobile, Nick knew it was almost time to depart. The Porsche was loaded in the ETV, the modifications perfect, and the final goodbyes imminent. Silence settled around them as they stood by the spacecraft, reflecting on the road they'd traveled together.

They looked back to survey the garage, marveling at its transformation. It was far more organized and inviting than it had been just months ago. Nick had painstakingly polished the once-cloudy windows and replaced some of the glass, now allowing a flood of natural light to illuminate the space. The weeds growing through the cracks had been pulled, the walls and window panes now painted, and the floor swept clean.

From his scarf pocket he presented Tee with a hand-drawn sketch of the finished Porsche he had envisioned months earlier, serving as a blueprint for the progress of the 996. "Call it Tee's Garage," he said as an afterthought.

"I will," Tee's voice cracked as he nodded back.

"Your father lives in you, Tee. Open this garage, make a good business, sir." His voice trembled. He fought his tears that threatened to spill. Tee nodded in silence.

In these quiet moments, Nick recounted the choices ahead—winning the race versus the ties on Earth. Each modification on the car felt like a metaphor for the tweaks he had to make to his own life—adjustments for survival, functionality, and speed. Yet, the transformation of his own heart mattered more.

Nick freed the spacecraft doors. Tee watched a mix of reverence and sadness in his posture. It was time.

"Take good care of things here, alright, Tee?" Then Nick revealed a Mountain Dew t-shirt he'd ordered for the boy.

Tee couldn't speak but dipped his chin, an edge of defiance against his emotions—as if challenging the universe to take away what they'd built. But his voice finally wavered as he pushed out the words. "Good luck, Nick."

"Thanks, Tee. For everything, mate."

As they released their handshake, Nick pondered all they had been through together. The laughter, the frustrations, the shared passion for the Porsche—all of it had created a bond that went beyond mere mechanics and lessons. It had become a source of companionship, a semblance of family that Nick had missed deeply.

Remaining stout, Nick continued, "There's something else. Tomorrow morning, Bee will arrive with a delivery. Tell her I had to leave for a long vacation and might not return. Ask her to open the package on the spot." He referred to an extra tennis racquet he'd purchased to replace the one she lent him. He would take it as a keepsake to remember their colorful friendship. It was now packed neatly with other mementos in his spacecraft.

Tee's face faltered as he absorbed the implications of Nick's words. "Nick, does this mean you're leaving for good?"

Nick nodded slowly, his throat tightening with the effort to maintain composure. "I'm afraid so, Tee. It's just something I have to do."

The reality of the situation hung thick in the air between them, each second passing like an eternity. Tee swallowed hard. It was as if they both wondered how they could possibly say goodbye to something that had become such a pivotal part of their lives. The garage, once a place of solitude and dust, had transformed into a space of learning and camaraderie, all because of Nick's presence.

"Okay, Nick," Tee finally said, struggling to keep his voice steady. "I'll make sure Bee gets the message. And... thank you for everything. I'll never forget what you've taught me."

Nick watched as Tee processed the instructions, the boy's face a mixture of emotion and determination. Each moment felt like a knife twisting in Nick's gut, the pain of impending separation more acute with every passing second.

The garage, aglow with the last light of day, seemed to hold its breath, mirroring the anticipation and sorrow that lingered within its walls. The tools, the workbench, the other finished projects—they all stood as silent witnesses to the bond forged between an alien mentor and a human apprentice.

Nick turned to leave, each step a reminder of the world he was leaving behind. He paused at the door, glancing back one last time at the boy, who stood amidst the evening shadows, a friend watching a friend take his leave.

As he looked back, the reality of his departure settled fully in his heart. The bonds formed here would stay with him always, a testament to the power of connection and the completeness of friendship, whether on Earth or among the stars. He knew this moment would etch itself deeply into his memory, forever a part of his journey.

Nick took a deep breath as he glanced inside the ETV, each memento a bittersweet reminder of the strange journey. He turned to Tee, "Hey, Tee," Nick started, trying to keep his voice steady. "Why didn't you ever ask me about the invisible trick, like I promised?"

Tee looked up, his blue eyes reflecting a quiet understanding. He pushed the hair from his forehead. "I just didn't want to ask you for anything else."

Nick's heart clenched at the boy's simple yet profound words. The urge to delay his departure tugged at him fiercely, questioning if the rules of his home planet were worth the heartache of leaving.

Taking a deep breath, Nick powered up his spacecraft. The engine purred to life with an alien hum, a sound that resonated with an otherworldly familiarity. He allowed himself a moment of pride, savoring the culmination of months of dedication and effort.

Nick stepped toward Tee, his motions deliberate as he began to walk him through the quantum mechanics of turning invisible. "Alright, the trick involves holding your breath. As long as you do, you'll remain unseen. But when you hold your breath, you add three things…" He showed him the secret.

Tee's eyes widened with a blend of excitement and disbelief. As Nick demonstrated, his form shimmered and then vanished, only to reappear moments later. Tee's expression shifted to one of amazement and gratitude as he understood the level of trust Nick had bestowed upon him.

Nick waited until Tee could mirror his actions and the process to ensure he could do the same. One last lesson from the mentor.

When Tee reappeared, without warning, he lunged forward and wrapped his arms around Nick. And Nick gently patted the boy's back, feeling the warmth and sincerity of the friendship.

He glanced back one last time to the back door, taking in the view of the dimly lit garage and every corner marked with memories of laughter, frustration, and triumph.

Tee stood alone, his silhouette framed against the golden evening light. The rays painted a picture of a world Nick had grown to love, one that had offered him a sense of belonging he'd never imagined possible.

The spacecraft's engines moaned softly, calling him to his return journey. Nick felt Tee's eyes on him, each second elongating as if to capture every facet of a loving farewell. Behind Tee's stoic expression lay the emotional realization that their time together had reached its end.

As Nick stood on the steps of the ETV, he saw his roadrunner friend dart across the backyard alongside its companion. The bird approached the spacecraft cautiously, maintaining a secure distance, cocked its head from side to side, and gawked curiously at Nick with its right eye.

"Newt," Nick said and dipped his chin once, "goodbye Newt."

The craft's door closed, sealing Nick within its confines. The purr of the engines grew louder, wrapping him in a cocoon of purpose and destiny. He placed his hand on the dashboard, feeling the pulsating energy coursing through the spacecraft.

He cast one last look at the world outside as he initiated the launch sequence. Tee's figure remained steadfast through the viewports, raising a hand in a silent goodbye. Nick reciprocated, his heart heavy yet filled with a promise to cherish those days. The spacecraft lifted off, and the familiar scenery of the garage and the surrounding desert began to blur into indistinct shapes, fading into the horizon.

The glowing dashboard contrasted with the encroaching darkness, a series of flashing lights, and the soft vibrations of the spacecraft's engines, signaling the end of his adventure on Earth.

Above all, he felt a mix of hope and sorrow. His mind raced with the joys of victory, the unforeseen paths ahead, a future of possibilities, and the lingering hope of someday finding a way back to those who had unknowingly given him a family.

The final echoes of the spacecraft faded into the quiet vastness of space, and Nick watched the garage, Tee's diminishing figure and the endless desert slowly dissolve into a palette of strewn, warm earth tones. As he waved a final goodbye, he held up his hand as if to proselytize, "I'm from the heavens," he cried out, trying to explain.

Then, Nick sling-shotted away.

Chapter Eleven

Completing the long journey through the cosmos and empty space, the ethereal beauty of Vetu's binary suns began to materialize. Yet part of Nick remained anchored to Earth. The decision to leave weighed heavily, intertwining love and sorrow with a renewed sense of identity.

He dedicated two full days to rejuvenating at home, allowing himself the emotional space to prepare for the upcoming race. He began to rethink his life, rooted in deeper self-reflection. As he regained some composure, he reached out to his friend Azi for coffee, barely reintegrating into his everyday routine while keeping his thoughts close to his friends back on Earth.

Nick's mood began to stabilize after the third day. Fresh thoughts of excitement began surfacing alongside reminiscent memories. As race day approached, it was a cunning process, but a crawling energy of passion finally remounted within him. He arrived at the track, enveloped by the roar of the buzzing crowd. The atmosphere thrummed with vibrant energy as banners danced joyfully in the steady breeze.

The brush noise of the warm moist wind gently passing his ears was a comforting pattern he'd forgotten. The summer solstice was at hand, a time when the sister suns drew perilously close to one another at the edge of the world, casting the dusky landscape in a deepening shade of mid-day amethyst twilight. All who attended savored the experience with genuine delight.

Stellar classics lined the pits of the racetrack, each proof of their owners' dedication and craftmanship. The drivers sported their colorful racing jumpsuits and circled their vehicles, meticulously examining every intricate detail and reveling in their workmanship, their egos flying high with the array of colored, galactical flags.

Nick inhaled, savoring the mix of octane, rubber, and his surroundings. This was the moment he'd been preparing for; broadcasting throughout his galaxy, it was the definitive factor in his anticipated status among friends and followers. The social pecking order of the racers wasn't merely about the race itself; It marked the difference between leading a lonely life and living a life abundant with friends and joy. Nick was striving to maintain a hopeful perspective, even as some of him remained tethered to Earth, detesting the social media likes and expectations.

He parked the GT2 as directed by the pit crews, the engine purring like a predator, and stepped out, trying to showcase an air of confidence that masked his fluttering nerves. He knew that every eye in the crowd was watching him, and each competitor gauging his stature.

Internally, he grappled with the weight of everything leading up to that moment. The countless hours of work, emotional investments, and friendships formed all seemed to hang out of balance. The consequences of losing, especially to Karl, were more than just the sting of defeat; they included the potential complete loss of respect and the shame of disappointing not just Vetu but himself as well.

He felt he owed it to Tee, Bee, Kiev, and the others far away to win. He did truly belong in this fierce, fast-paced world. But he hoped today, he wasn't destined to remain an outsider, unable to fully integrate into either world.

The racers 'oohed' and 'aahed' over the classic GT2 with their various ga-ga faces and googly eyes. His Porsche mirrored the heavens in the twilight; the classic craft was truly a masterpiece.

Acme AI had been powered off since his arrival on Vetu. He acknowledged her invaluable assistance in restoring the car yet hesitated to rely on her during the race, fearing it might jeopardize everything.

Walking through the crowd at the pit, he spotted Karl standing with his Porsche 997. They exchanged glares, tension building between them. His Turbo was a beastly racer, which they both understood. The smell of rubber and oil surrounding him was a similar flavor to the old Earthly garage, and Nick thought of a witty jab. "With your white face stubble, you look like Santa Claus in that red sleigh, mate."

Karl crinkled his forehead and curled his cigar with one finger, clearly puzzled. The confusion in his eyes yielded Nick a small, private delight. Tee had taught him about Christmas, a human tradition, and its significance.

The race announcer's voice resonated powerfully, heralding each competitor with enthusiasm. A dazzling array of classic cars graced the track, including Azi's formidable BMW M6, a ghostly white Ferrari Modena 360 with quartz yellow-tinted headlights, an aggressive Mercedes AMG, and other high-performance machines like Lotus and Lamborghini.

There were many classic racers from the Creamy Way and various other galaxies. The S7 Kelvinator and the Lozier Racer both splendid creations from planet Quantis—unyielding competitors with an edge. The lineup also featured remarkable racers from Kissel Motors, Kaiser-Frazer Corp., Moon Motor Corp., and REO, as well as iconic names like Nash, Hudson, and Fritz—all vibrant classics meticulously enhanced from diverse star systems.

Adding to this remarkable array was a 2005 DeLorean SRS from planet X18, a tribute to John DeLorean's legacy on Earth. An entrepreneur named Squaw Daimler had infiltrated Earth to acquire an original DeLorean, relocating it to his home world and redesigning it using extraterrestrial engineering principles, all while preserving the iconic gullwing doors and stainless steel body. That year, he celebrated the astounding sale of half a million reproduced units on his home planet.

"Windowwws Dowwwn!" The announcer shouted the cardinal rule just before any race launched. The mounted bullhorn speakers echoed from the tall wooden poles strategically placed throughout the stadium. The unique pitch was like an echo from an empty room, yet the bodies in the packed stadium absorbed the vibrations.

The crowd erupted in cheers and jeers, each shout amplifying the pressure in the air. Nick moved toward his car, his heart pounding with the rhythm of the motors surrounding him. He buckled the red five-point harness seat belt while mentally pacing through the victory.

He went so far as to imagine the shelf in his modern flat he would decorate with the winning gold medallion and platinum car show cup, which he would place alongside his helmet.

Sitting inside the Porsche, Nick felt the weight of the multiverse on his shoulders. The crowd's energy was electrifying, fueling both his excitement and anxiety. At that moment, under the wavering flags of Vetu and chanting sea of voices, the stakes were at their highest.

There he was, lined up at the cusp of destiny, ready to prove himself. The roar of more engines filled the air as they each keyed their ignitions. The mechanical might burst across the racetrack and bleachers as the custom speedsters lined up at the broad, checkered starting line. Nick sat in the driver's seat of his restored wonder, the vibration of the engine thrumming through his body. His glare-free goggles were strapped around his head, and his helmet was secured with a tightly pulled chin strap and chrome buckle.

As the announcer initiated the countdown, the importance of the day pulsed in his blood. The crowd's excited murmurs and cheers created a distant, scattered haze, a mist of vibrations as he focused on the starting flag. His heart pounded as his fingers tightly gummed around the steering wheel with practiced determination. Still uncertain, he reached for the glove compartment and activated Acme Amy.

The moment before the announcer called the race to begin, his gaze drifted to a photograph taped to the dashboard—a picture featuring Bee and Tee during their recent adventure. The picture captured the three of them proudly gathered at the iconic Las Vegas sign along the bustling Strip. In the photograph, Bee's radiant smile seemed to reach him as she gave a thumbs-up, while Tee grinned ear to ear, his hair wind-tousled and carefree.

Nick's thoughts flashed to Tee, the eager apprentice with a bright future, probably in the garage at that moment, and Bee, whose smiles, warmth, and perseverance probably clinched her the women's ITF tennis title.

He knew that the race wasn't just a quest for victory; it was a test of everything he'd built and the relationships he'd formed. He felt the cool metal of the hydraulic control mount on his outer thigh—a reminder of the hours he and Tee spent crafting custom parts. His gaze drifted to the passenger seat, where Bee's tennis racquet was twisted tightly into the seatbelt.

The flag dropped. Cars exploded forward with intimidating thunder, slow at first, clacking and bursting with lightning flames. Tires began screeching against the asphalt, leaving behind the smoky, biting whiff of burning rubber. Nick felt the routine surge of adrenaline rushing through his veins, a feeling that had hooked him on racing all these years.

The world outside his windows blurred into a time-lapsed exposure of colors, streaming with the crowd's enthusiastic frenzy and seamlessly with the checkered red and white barrier walls of the track.

Nick conversed with the Acme system to calm his nerves, the smooth voice of the AI filling the confines. "996 GT2 Suspension—optimal. Tire pressure—optimal. Engine performance—optimal," she reported. The first curve loomed ahead, and Nick deftly maneuvered the wheel, downshifting into second gear, stacking the RPMs with the upward sound of a zing. He felt the Porsche respond as if it were an extension of his body. His internal dialogue buzzed with tension but also with the comforting familiarity of every turn and twist of the car he'd spent months perfecting.

"Careful, your tires are still cold," the Acme AI advised.

He looked in the rearview mirror at his goofy head crammed into the helmet, then unnecessarily turned toward the glovebox when he spoke, "Yeah, I know, I know."

"Would you like me to stop giving advice altogether, sir?" Acme asked.

"Eha, well, eha, no! I *do* want some. Just hold your peace, Amy!"

"You don't like me," she continued.

"Oh my gosh! Please, not now! We'll talk about it later! I *do* like you!"

"Fine."

He glanced in his rearview mirror, catching a glimpse of Karl's Porsche. The sight of it immediately fueled his competitive edge. Memories of their century-long rivalry surfaced—each race, each contentious encounter forming layers of animosity. Karl's attempt to overtake him in the curve was expected. The cheater also played aggressively, and Nick had learned to anticipate his audacity.

With a swift maneuver, Nick avoided Karl's advance, feeling air pump into the suspension and stiffen under his command. There was no room for error now. He'd dreamed of this moment, visualizing it during the long nights in the dusty ghost town garage, Tee and Bee's laughter echoing in his mind as they encouraged him through his work.

Bee's image appeared in his thoughts, her hazel eyes filled with determination as she'd challenged him to tennis matches that tested his human agility and overall resilience. The sparkle of the tennis racquet he kept in the car—a reminder of those moments—gleamed in the passenger seat as twinkles of light from the track passed through the Porsche windows. "Focus," he reminded himself, drawing strength from the memories of the past six months.

Nick accelerated out of the first curve, his heart racing to the engine's revs. Each modification he'd made to the Porsche passed through his mind in rapid succession—the aftermarket exhaust, the custom suspension, the fine-tuning that had pushed the car's limits. The hours he'd spent tutoring the boy and forming a bond with both him and the car.

As he thundered down the track, the tension of the race heightened with every passing second. The spectators' faces blended into an ocean of anticipation, fueling Nick's resolve. The asphalt track beneath him was stained with the ghosts and gods of grease and bore witness to the reality of relentless pursuits.

"All systems optimal. Keep current pace," Acme AI's voice advised, piercing through the cacophony of thoughts and other noises. Nick's mind was a combat zone, each second a wrestle between the drive to win and the emotional turmoil of permanent separation from his loving friends.

Recalling the first time he'd laid eyes on the modest, off-grid garage hidden in a Nevada canyon, Nick couldn't help but feel a pang of nostalgia. The structure had been on the verge of collapse, just waiting for someone to breathe new life into it, much like Nick's relationship with racing. It symbolized renewal, struggle, and a second chance—a chance now coursing through his veins as he hugged every corner and turn of the race.

He felt an overwhelming sense of kinship with Tee, who reminded him of his own youthful ambitions, and Bee, who brought color to his gray days and laughter to his lonely nights.

Nick's grip tightened on the aluminum wheel, his knuckles whitening as he approached another sharp turn. He refocused on the present, feeling every vibration and hearing every rumble, fully attuned to the Porsche's performance. The modifications, the camaraderie, and the anticipation of the race—all coalesced into a singular moment of raw, unyielding determination.

As he sped past the checkpoint, maintaining his position against Karl, Nick felt more connected to his purpose than ever before. The crowd roared with enthusiasm, creating a backdrop that pulsed like a heartbeat amidst the thunder of engines, driving the energy of the race. Each note of the moment was a testament to his journey—a confluence of dedication, love, and the relentless pursuit of a dream.

While Nick kept a keen eye on Karl, Azi must have unleashed his supercharger as he surged ahead in the BMW M6, claiming the top spot in the race.

Nick kept a watchful eye on Karl behind. His 997 tailed like a predator, but Nick closely maintained second place around every banked curve, his polished aluminum wheels propelling over the smooth slopes of the hot track.

Memories of past races on Vetu flooded Nick's mind again—the late nights spent fine-tuning vehicles, the melting sensation of rubber on asphalt, and the bitter taste of erroneous defeats that Karl had so often forced upon him. Karl was relentless, but Nick had learned the importance of precision and strategy from those cheating trials. He wouldn't let Karl get the better of him again.

Racing out of the next curve, he found a honed sense of focus on the long straightaway. Victory was not just an endpoint but a passage woven into every experience, decision, and relationship. He upshifted into sixth gear. The ghostly figures of past races faded, leaving only the resolute present. Drawing a breath, Nick braced himself, committed to seeing it through—not just for the triumph but to finish what he'd begun.

Nick's fingers danced over the controls, slightly testing the hydraulic airbag system and lowering the car by some millimeters. He turned up the volume to the head unit. The

Acme AI responded instantly, her smooth digital voice cutting through the throaty roar of the engines. "Optimizing suspension performance for the next stretch," she announced.

Nick's bond with the car ran deep. He'd poured his heart into this machine. He'd given it everything he had—every ounce of energy and thought from his soul, transferred into revolutionizing it into a formidable racer.

As Acme AI recalibrated the settings, Nick couldn't help but feel a flicker of camaraderie for the unit—an uneasy friendship born of chance and necessity. He wasn't sure why he'd decided to power it on that day. Probably because it reminded him of his friends. The old, hated technology that once belonged to Karl's company was now his ally, 17.0.

After tiresome concentration during the lengthy race, the cars finally clocked forty laps. Nick had lapped some of the racers now spread around the track. Among the other frontrunners, he skillfully maneuvered through a smoking and twisting crash, then zipped past the black M6. He gave his two-fingered perfunctory salute to Azi, then clinched the coveted first-place position.

The audience erupted in a frenzy of laughter and cheers as the announcer echoed throughout the stadium about how the Old Dog had seized control of the competition. But the crowd's laughter turned boastfully optimistic as Karl also outpaced and zipped past Azi, still only trailing Nick.

But with a sudden jolt, the 996 sputtered. "Warning," Acme AI alerted him.

"*Errrnt, errrnt, errrnt.*" A nasty buzzing sound ensued.

"Slight mechanical issue detected," she called out.

A cold wave of doubt washed over Nick, and his heart sank. Mechanical failures had cost him races, this moment haunted by the bitter knowledge of defeat. His mind raced, recalling the diagnostics Acme AI had provided in the past. He recalled each component he'd replaced, each system he'd meticulously calibrated. He knew the job was complete, whether it was a busted fan belt or a faulty sensor.

Acme AI's loud voice pierced his thoughts, diagnosing the issue, "Jam in the Numeric racing throw shifter."

Nick's hands moved with practiced speed as he pried open the car's shifter u-plate shroud surrounding the manual shift knob on the console. His car lurched back, with Karl swiftly taking the lead on him. Nick pushed the accelerator, and the car responded to his command, allowing him to maintain his speed on the next straightaway.

While keeping Azi at bay, a rush of adrenaline surged through him. The crowd went wild. Ten more laps were left until the finish line. He would need to repair the issue in real-time or lose the race.

After accessing the shift compartment, he examined the connections and fasteners to identify the problem. To his astonishment, he discovered a pizza crust wedged inside the mechanism. After swiftly removing the encumbrance, he felt the Porsche leap back into action, regaining its former momentum.

Familiar scenes from Earth flashed before him—his eager apprentice helping with the repairs, the green Mountain Dews, and thoughts of Bee's championship tennis match, which he painfully had not attended. Visions of their faces fueled his determination, propelling him forward. All three of them were winners, chiseled from the same rock.

The track stretched ahead, a ribbon of opportunity bordered by roaring spectators and snapping flags. His hands remained steady on the wheel as he expertly navigated the curves. He drowned out the cheers and jeers of the crowd mingling with the relentless hum of the engines. His focus zeroed in on the open road, concentrating on Karl's snarling presence.

Karl maintained his lead, Nick trailing closely but unable to overtake. Each burst of acceleration was followed by Karl's defensive maneuvers.

His grip tightened, and his eyes narrowed. The mechanical issue had been a hiccup, a reminder of the fragility and resilience of all machinery. With every passing second, his connection to the Porsche and his memories comforted his spirit, pushing him to maintain his lead over Azi, who now battled with the ghostly white Ferrari Modena. Now just three laps away, the finish line drew closer with every calculated maneuver.

With every bank and slope of the track building toward his new life, he felt the best of him was due to arrive. Nick went deeper, his confidence growing and his focus sharpening as he navigated. The end of the race was near, and he was ready to throw his final card.

As the finish line appeared before him, the pressure of the moment descended like a storm. His muscles coiled with tension, his heart hammering against his ribs. On the last turn of the track, he rubbed bumpers with Karl as he surged parallel with the 997 for the final straightaway.

The two cars streaked down the final stretch, neck and neck. Nick's grip tightened on the steering wheel, sweat slicking his palms. Acme AI's voice echoed in his ears, providing critical feedback and telling Nick to push the car to its max.

Karl glanced over. He threw his head back in a burst of mocking laughter and let his wicked tongue flap freely as their eyes locked.

At the last moment, with a swift motion, Nick activated the hydraulic airbags, which raised the car's rear body fifteen centimeters. Then, looking again at the photograph taped to the dashboard, his finger aggressively punched the red-mounted nitrous oxide button by the shifter, feeling an immediate surge of power. A pop of air sounded from the motor and crackling from the rear. The butt of the car buckled with immense force as the torque squashed it down to the asphalt. The GT2 rocketed forward, the blustering engine melding with the thunderous exhaust echoed from the racetrack walls igniting the roar of anticipation from the crowd.

He surged at eight thousand RPMs, leaving Karl's 997 trailing but only inches behind. The contempt on Karl's face was unmistakable—a silent showdown steeped in their longstanding rivalry. Nick's emotions of determination swelled with excitement, a hint of fear and anger.

The finish line flashed by in a blur of checkers and a mirage of heat, and Nick then waned the racer after he crossed, a slim but indisputable win!

He looked just in time to see Karl's disbelieving expression twist with frustration and Azi place third. Triumph surged through him, a rush of elation so intense it nearly stole his breath. Then he watched the others cross in his mirror. The Ferrari, the DeLorean, the Lamborghini, and others.

Nick's victory smile rested as his astonishment settled in—the race was over. He had won the most important race of the century.

As the cheers swelled to a crescendo for many moments and then began to fade some decibels, the announcer called his name, "Nick R. Bates!" omitting the tag Old Dog. Nick let the noise of the crowd wash into his heart.

He continued around the racetrack on his prized victory lap, now filled with echoes of celebration. He was satisfied knowing that his presence was revived for good, or at least for centuries to come.

When he stopped in the pit and emerged from his Porsche, he looked again at the joyful crowd. They were throwing a steady stream of roses toward him and cheering with all the excitement they'd extracted that day.

He unzipped his racing suit and was greeted by the lanyard staff from the WCACCV2, who popped a green bottle of vintage bubbly and sprayed him down. The cameras flashed as they removed the wet golden label, pressed it onto his forehead, adorned his neck with the gold medallion, and followed other time-honored traditions. It was a rare moment on Vetu that reminded him of the warmth of human kindness.

He recounted Earth and how he was just a visitor from the heavens, bound by rules he neither made nor fully understood. He thought of its chaotic beauty, the friends he'd made, the connections forged in the crucible of his mission.

He wondered if the camaraderie of the race would transform into actual revived friendships and linger in his heart, or would it fade, dulled by the passage of celestial days and unfavorable energy that had stoked into their culture. The thought twisted in his mind, a bitter contemplation amidst the sweetness of triumph and frenzy.

Victorious, he stood by his Porsche, absorbing the snapshots, fading cheers, and magnitude of what lay ahead. The thrill of his win blended with a need for solemn reflection. Mysteriously, he found himself wanting to be alone. He knew he needed time to contemplate.

Nick's mind swirled with thoughts of friendship, loyalty, and a love he'd never expected to find on a dusty blue planet in another galaxy so far from home. Tee's eager face, Bee's infectious laughter. How easily they had welcomed him into their lives. But the stakes were clear. His return to Vetu meant leaving behind a piece of his heart on Earth forever.

His gaze swept over the crowd one last time, noting the spectators' smiles and ecstasy. Their expressions reflected both the sweetness of his victory and a sharp reminder of how quickly their sentiment could shift.

He pondered if the galactic race and all its glory would ever compare to the simple joy of a human connection.

Chapter Twelve

Nick's victory was claimed. His skills and resilience, honed from years of experience, proved the Old Dog was never truly old. He no longer concerned himself with his social status or the empty pursuit of fame and followers. Yet his triumph that day carried the burden of an uncertain future.

He stayed alone that weekend. The Vetu solstice had passed, though those days remained short, filled only with twilight. He stayed near artificial light, as others did in the hemisphere's tradition, some by meandering through the local town's carnival, a kaleidoscopic of whirling lights.

Arrays of all colors danced off the glass buildings, creating a shimmering tapestry that flickered with the pulsating rhythms of the carnival rides. The air was alive with the buzz of conversation and occasional cheer.

Children with bright glowing necklaces and curious eyes darted past him, his solitary meditative state absorbing the laughter and pouting faces, which all weaved new thoughts into his mind.

As he strolled past kiosks and blankets spread with souvenirs, his eyes were drawn to a pinboard of vibrant, lustrous fliers fluttering nearby. Among them was a post containing a picture of himself, featuring bold letters that read, "Car God: Nick R. Bates." And beneath, there was subtext that read, "Washed-up racer from Planet Vetu wins galactical race and car show of the century with beastly Porsche 996." At the very bottom, in small letters, it read, "Join our club, WCACCV2." A picture showcased an action shot of Nick— the lanyard crew lacing him with victory.

He noticed another bold, luminescent orange announcement that reminded him of Tee's dirt bike. "Off-Road Race Qualifier—Mystical Dunes—Planet F5—Next Year!" An elaborate hologram of speed and excitement played out beneath the text, where his image appeared again—a snapshot of Nick proudly displaying his medallion and platinum cup. However, it wasn't the flashy display or his image that gripped Nick's heart. The words themselves directed his thoughts toward a future of possibilities.

For a moment, everything around him faded. He was once more on Earth, navigating the dusty roads of the Mojave winds in his trusty 996. Tee's exuberant laughter filled the car as Bee's animated storytelling intertwined with the deep scent of the garage. He heard the steady voice of Kiev, sharing sage advice between thoughtful sips of his ever-present loose-leaf green tea. He remembered the intimate gatherings, the lunches, feisty Darla, the spontaneous road trips, and the silence over sunset vistas, each memory a precious jewel of his journey.

The memory of a city carnival he had once attended with Bee flashed vividly. The scattered lights, the aroma of popcorn, and the sounds of joyful screams from the rides. They had shared cotton candy, laughing about their sticky fingers as they wandered through the colorful chaos. At one point, Bee had quickly pressed her tacky finger to his face, marking a goo of pink sugar that pulled on his cheek with her finger before it released to snap back into place.

Under the night skies, their conversation flowed effortlessly, a connection that felt both exhilarating and frightening. Bee's warm, hazel eyes held a promise of perhaps something Nick hadn't fully allowed himself to explore.

The unspoken expectations to excel and to rise above, in this era, twice, had crafted walls around Nick's spirit. He had now been seen as a maverick for the second time in his community around the galaxy. However, that isolation and relentless drive slowly eroded the core of who he truly wanted to be.

The festive lights blurred momentarily as he absorbed the buzzing crowds around him. This new option ahead seemed to grow with every passing moment, drawing him into an intricate web of excitement and fear. If he played his cards correctly, the new contest would be an opportunity—not for social standing but to revisit Earth. It was a chance to mitigate the finality of a door closing on his friends, who had become his family.

Nick swallowed, his throat dry. The sounds of the carnival felt dulled, as though he were underwater—disconnected and adrift. He began walking toward the exit, each step heavy with the influx of memories and the weight of unresolved desire.

Pulling himself away from the bustling carnival, Nick headed toward his Porsche, which reflected the lights at the carnival's subdued perimeter. The night air wrapped around him, a mix of cool relief and bitter solitude. With every footfall, he could hear the unspoken voices of his local friends and feel the tug of their shared history, begging him to reconsider.

The 996's aggressive stance seemed almost mournful, its black chrome exhaust tips protruding from its gilled bumper. He slipped inside, the scent of leather and aluminum attempting to ground him, but his thoughts remained a choppy sea of possibilities. His fingers gripped the steering wheel as his eyes fell again on the orange flier he'd unconsciously brought with him.

The reality of yet another choice settled over him like a suffocating blanket. After all, he could leave Vetu and all of his glory to build another Porsche and start all over again.

A colossal wave surged within him—fear, longing, and a profound sadness that seemed to seep into his bones. The carnival's vibrant cheerfulness felt like a cruel contrast to his desires within.

Nick allowed himself a single, weary sigh. The possible new journey ahead would demand everything he had. The choice wasn't about glitz or glory but about who he wanted to be and where he truly felt he belonged.

As the vibrant hues of the carnival lights receded in his rearview mirror, the roar of his engine comforted him, as it frequently did during moments of solitude and contemplation.

He envisioned standing with his faraway friends in the Milky Way, in front of those beautiful, dirty garage windows, and telling them every detail of the race. He could share the truth with Bee, for better or worse. He knew she would, at very least, always be his friend, even if a romance between them was unattainable. The camaraderie of those spontaneous road trips seemed to be all that mattered. Bee's tuneful laughter, a sound that made the desert air feel more lively, felt almost tangible.

Tee, with his boyish grin and the daring stunts on his dirt bike he ended in laughter and skids into the dust. He contemplated possible ways to return to Earth and the implications of staying permanently. Maybe he could run the garage business with Tee, selling motor overhauls and repairs to the nearby city's inhabitants.

Nick's playlist filled the car's interior—a mix from Bee that started with Ozzy Osbourne's song "Mama, I'm Coming Home." Nick could clearly see Bee's animated expression and how her eyes lit up with a spark every time the chorus hit. The melody tugged at him, intensifying the already overwhelming flood of feelings. Each verse felt like a shared memory; the sound carried the laughter, joy, and unwavering sense of adventure that had defined their time together.

In his mind's eye, Nick revisited the many recommendations from Keiv, the leather, paint, and tint shops he had visited. Keiv was always a fount of wisdom amid the chaos. His steady and reassuring presence had been a silent anchor, guiding Nick with patience and expertise. They had spent time talking at the dealership and attending a few Porsche Club of America events with the crowds of enthusiasts.

Even Rod at RS Customs. Sure, he had been late with the repairs and never returned Nick's phone calls, but it was okay because he was Chinese. Chinese, like the food Nick shared with Bee during her surprise visit. And Rod did a great job on the paint correction and the other modifications.

Nick's grip on the steering wheel tightened as the emotional weight began to settle with no escape. Leaving these cherished memories felt like a betrayal, a severance of a part of his soul that had found solace and belonged on Earth. The idea of remaining in the isolation of Vetu, where he was measured by his achievements and external possessions, tore at him. He had spent so long yearning for a sense of connection.

As the Porsche glided through the picturesque landscapes of his planet, the deep-colored suns plunged to the horizon as far as they would go, casting shadows that stretched like phantoms across his life. The array of amethyst sparkles heightened the surreal beauty of the world around him, yet it only amplified the melancholy he felt. Each mile brought him closer to the impending decision.

The car's stereo continued to play, with each song feeling like a chapter of his story on Earth. The fear of missing out on a life filled with new adventures, people, places, and things tightened the knot in his stomach. It dawned on him that as precious as they were, those memories might be all he would have to hold onto for the rest of his life.

When Nick finally pulled into his dark driveway, the purple haze that bathed his Porsche seemed almost poetic. He sat there for a moment longer, staring at the flier and then glancing back at the pinned photograph, feeling a pang of sorrow so deep it hurt.

Leaving the Porsche behind would be difficult, but it was the people, the relationships, and the memories intertwined with the car that he feared losing most. The driveway felt cold and empty as he swung the car door closed. As it clacked shut, the last tuning ping of the metal accentuated the depth of emptiness that echoed around him.

Nick tried to focus on the comfort of the memories. Tomorrow awaited its own set of challenges and possible farewells, but tonight, in the quiet of the falling night, Nick knew those moments from Earth would stay with him, etched into his very being.

On Sunday morning, he arrived at the Cars and Coffee event, sporting his new Porsche houndstooth scarf. A sea of genuine smiles and accolades from his friends immediately enveloped him as he parked the Porsche in his reserved space. *'New Tricks,'* they called him as he waded through the crowd of a hundred members to find Azi, his friends, and a cup of joe.

Nick moved through the crowd, his heart heavy with the weight of an impending speech. He absorbed the scene. The lovely scent of the freshly cut, endless green lawn he'd forgotten about and the lined-up colored coffee mugs that permanently displayed the individual members' names. Their cups often matched their scarves or polo shirts.

"You're a god!" his buddy, '*Two*,' called out from a few feet away as Nick strolled. Two was given that name because he always had a two-car fleet—two racers in his garage at all times.

"New Trix!" his longtime friend, 'Spectator,' hollered. He talked a good race but didn't track his car much. He preferred to keep it clean and just watch from the sidelines mostly, with his thick Coke bottle spectacles, of course.

Then there was 'Private,' who had only seven followers on social media despite his four thousand picture posts. He claimed to prefer a private life, which Nick and the crew found hard to believe.

Then there was 'Coffee Hound.' She was a female who wanted men just as much as she wanted coffee. "The god of cars and racing!" she whispered into Nick's ear as she made a pass.

"Oh, hey there, Nick. I mean, New Trix. Nice race. I'm hanging out with Ryan." 'Checker' went along with whatever everybody else was doing. He talked slowly and calmly in a soft monotone. He was a shy guy. Nick had known him for a long time but didn't know why they called him that name.

Then there was 'Ryan,' simply 'Ryan,' for whom they could never think of a nickname. He was just—normal.

The aroma of freshly brewed coffee from the steel cauldrons mingled with the scent of motors and motorheads' cologne, the grass, and the vibrations of animated conversations that buzzed. Nick paused, taking mental snapshots of the colored faces he'd grown accustomed to—each line and curve a culmination of his unique home planet.

They possessed goodness in their hearts; however, their existence lacked the vibrancy and warmth that life on Earth offered. Their demeanor was frosty, reflecting their nature. Their happiness felt limited, untouched by the warmth of an emotion they had never experienced.

Nevertheless, they cherished one another in their own way. He mused that if only their brains could match a human heart, they could all live happily on one planet.

Nick found and approached Azi, of course—or 'Z,' the only one among them who insisted on a nickname change. This practice was impossible within the group. Nick strictly called him 'Slicker' in secret and rarely. It was usually only when Azi insisted, but Nick hesitated for fear of being chastised by the others. "Hey, Nick," he said as a huddle of friends formed a roasting. "Remember that time we drove my racer out to the ocean and got stuck in the sand? You were convinced we'd never get home!" he teased, widening his eyes with memories.

Nick laughed, enjoying the moment. "Yeah, I thought we'd be out there until the next millennium."

Then a newcomer named 'Peckerwood' broke into the group, "I love your 996, mate! It looks very aggressive."

A profound sadness seeped into Nick's soul as his friends recounted more stories. The memories, once a source of joy, were now bittersweet echoes of a life he thought to leave behind.

Beneath his forced smile, a new storm of emotions churned within him. He remained deeply connected to Planet Vetu, a connection to his friends forged over many years, even if it was one that lacked the functionality or vitality it truly deserved. His friends, unaware of his looming departure, shared stories and laughter, oblivious to the secret he carried.

Nick felt his resolve harden as the fresh morning faded into afternoon. Gathering his courage, he stepped onto a makeshift stage with a podium, clearing his throat to catch the massive crowd's attention. The lively chatter slowly dissipated, replaced by their curious gazes.

"Ehh, hey, everyone," Nick began, then let out a sigh.

"Earth! Bruce Springsteen! Flip yeah, Nick!" A voice yelled, and the crowd's laughter broke out.

"Best racer in the Creamy Way!" Another voice yelled.

Nick delivered an inspiring speech, expressing his immense pride in being both a member and the president of the WCACCV2. He extended his heartfelt gratitude to the racers and supporters of the recent galactic race. His words focused on perseverance, and he included humorous anecdotes, such as how his tennis lessons contributed to his ultimate victory on the track. As he concluded, he paused, and a silence fell over the crowd.

"I need to tell you all something important."

Their faces were mixed with confusion and concern at his wavering tone. Nick's heart pounded in his chest as he struggled to find the right words. He felt his friends' eyes boring into him, silently urging him to continue.

"I... I've decided to leave," he said, his voice breaking. "There is another race on F5," he pushed out of his mouth. "Eh, a year from now," he continued. "It's at Mystical Dunes, off-road. I know it's a ways off, but I-I'm going back to Earth until then."

"You can't! You'll lose your car!" A voice from the crowd yelped.

"I, I... know. I'm resigning as the president of WCACCV2. Azi can take over from here." It was all he could do to push out the words and keep a firm voice.

There was a collective gasp, and a myriad of emotions flashed across the faces before him—shock, sadness, and disbelief. Nick's vision blurred with unshed tears as he forced himself to meet their eyes, his own heart breaking at his betrayal of their friendship. Lastly, he looked directly at his friend Azi.

"I know this is sudden, and I wish I could stay," he continued, his voice thick with emotion. Azi didn't appear surprised due to the numerous phone calls they'd previously shared. "But I have unresolved camaraderie back on Earth that I can't ignore anymore. This Porsche... it was never just about the car for me. I've realized it was about the journey, the friends I made, all of you, our shared love for cars—you inspired me to adventure."

He tried not to discount them. After all, they had been an essential part of his life. Even though they were shallow and two-dimensional, they had brilliant minds and fascinating ideas.

The carefree spark in Azi's eyes was gone when Nick looked back at him. Nick fought back tears as he reached into his pocket and pulled out the key to his beloved black stallion. His hand trembled as he offered it to Azi, the gesture carrying the weight of finality.

"Z, I'm entrusting you with this car and the WCACCV2. Take care of it and remember all the good times we shared."

"Are you sure you want to do this, Nick? We'll miss you. I mean, I'll miss you."

"We'll talk by interstellar video, mate, and I'll visit from time to time." Nick helped him cope.

"It just won't be the same without you. But, however, you're happy, brother." Azi's tone was lighter than it had been all year.

"Give me adventure or give me death!" Nick said with fervor and intensity into the microphone. He conveyed confidence aloud so Azi and the others wouldn't try to convince him otherwise.

In the past, Azi seemed to believe he knew what was best for everyone else's lives. Nick loved Azi, but the unsolicited advice was a constant thorn in his side, irritating him for a hundred years. However, Azi embraced him, and the crowd initiated an appropriate wave of applause.

Then they stood in silence, confused. The impact of Nick's words settled over them like a heavy fog. He stepped down from the podium, and the crowd's murmurs began a distant buzz in his ears. The reality of his decision weighed on him, and the pack of friends he had known for years mingled painfully with the cold finality of goodbye.

Nick shook hands, with some nods of appreciation, and embraced others. He bid farewell to Spectator, Two, and all of the others. Peckerwood approached with a sense of regret, expressing his disappointment and how he'd witnessed Nick's victory at the race and now missed the chance to connect with him because he had just joined their car club.

As he walked away, each step felt like a thousand miles. His mind raced with memories—road trips, late-night conversations, and the rooted vibrations of his home planet. But an identity transcended worlds. He felt a lump in his throat, blending with the bittersweet emotions that threatened to overwhelm him.

Azi lingered nearby. "Well, if you decide to stay. I'll travel with you. We can go to F5 together," he paused, "and get one of those baguettes." Azi pitched him an idea that he, himself would find adventurous, but not Nick.

This parting was more than a change in location. It was the end of an era, a severing of old ties that had come to define him. He might have won the race and regained his social standing, but amidst the receding voices of friends he cherished, Nick knew he had sacrificed something immensely comfortable and traded it for the opportunity of something far more profound.

Nick reached into the passenger side of his Porsche racer, took a lasting look at its glossy interior trim, and grabbed the orange-printed flier listing the off-road car race. He gently lifted the photograph from the dashboard. Then he reached in further to open the glove compartment. Its cold latch touched with memories and adventures.

Nick glanced back at Azi, who was now absorbed in his mobile device, holding a pencil in his hand he'd retrieved from his nearby M6. Nick paused for a moment to reflect with sincere gratitude, then bid farewell—conversing with Acme Amy, expressing appreciation for the invaluable assistance she had offered in securing his victory in the race. He mentioned that communication between them might be sparse in the near future. Carefully, he detached the Acme box and tucked it firmly beneath one arm while securing Bee's tennis racquet from the front seat in the other.

As he gradually stepped away from the gathering, Azi followed him, handing him a small paper note. When he unfolded the note with trembling hands, Ara Spaceman's address stared back at him. Amy's Daughter on Planet F5. He hugged Azi—a farewell for now, a bit of sorrow and swirling feelings of nostalgia and excitement mixed in his chest.

"Maybe I'll visit the Milky Way to see you, mate. How are the women there? I mean the hotels. I hear they have good hotels. I hear they have one called the Four Seasons." Azi's tone turned hopeful. "I'll miss you!" he finished. Nick informed Azi that he was welcome to visit any time. "You've been a good friend. We'll always be friends," Azi finished.

"No doubt, my friend." Nick felt a pang of loss, knowing this could be one of the last times he would see them and Vetu in this light. It was far, and frequent visits would not be entirely possible.

After a taxi ride home he programmed Ara Spaceman's address into his GPS device. The amber characters flickered across the windows of his classic ETV, and the animated compass spun to life, the app showing a clear route to planet F5. Nick took a deep breath, slowly releasing the weight of the past days. After one last look at the flier, he clamped his eyes shut briefly, summoning the courage to move forward.

The rheostatic sounds of the space engines hummed to life as he set the accepted course for planet F5. He nestled back into the pilot seat and stared at the clear, violet, star-studded sky beyond the windshield. The cosmos stretched infinitely before him, an expanse of possibilities and echoes from the past.

His thoughts drifted as the spacecraft glided through the galaxy, the harsh glow of the control panel illuminating his green face. Vivid memories flooded his mind as he contemplated how he'd arrived at this pivotal moment and finally made this choice.

Within a few hours, he arrived at planet F5. Nick held his breath at the sight of the bustling, dirty cityscape below. The architecture blended older technology and organic forms, with towers illuminated in muted colors, creating a scene his Vetu friends frequently shunned but his earthly friends could only dream of. His classic spacecraft descended gracefully, navigating the densely packed urban maze. The GPS directed him to a sleek, minimalist building embedded in the heart of the city, its reflective surfaces gleaming under the star system it shared with Vetu.

Stepping out, Nick approached the entrance to Ara's building with a sense of trepidation. Both the thrumming energy of the city and the dusty film seeped into his nostrils, invigorating and disorienting. As he pushed open the tall, intricately carved wooden door, he stepped into a world of organic forms, harmoniously shaped with roots and tech to complement the soft glow of ambient light, a distinct feeling of the planet and its various buildings and residential mid-rises.

Nick gripped the Acme box while informing the receptionist of who he was there to visit, prompting a screened call to Ara's apartment. Then reality surfaced, Ara might not be home—perhaps at work or even away on vacation. It crossed his mind that she might not even be on this planet. He regretted his impulsiveness, realizing he should have reached out to her before arriving. Thoughts raced through his mind about possibly tracking her down at her workplace.

He looked at the time on his mobile device. It was just past dinner time. He doubted she was actually on vacation, as most residents of F5 struggled with work, tethered to their unstable economy. But Azi was thorough, surely not adventurous, but reliable. Just then, the receptionist broke the silence.

"Mr. Nick R. Bates is here to see you. He has a delivery," she announced, holding a glass phone receiver to her ear.

There was a faint voice of melody from the other end of the line.

"She'll be down in a few moments, Mr. Bates," the receptionist spoke while ending the phone call.

A wave of relief surged through Nick with an undercurrent of nervousness. Not from the staring receptionist, who now irritated him.

Moments later, the elevator's ding echoed, and a woman emerged from its double wooden doors. Her long, creamy, honey-blonde hair instantly evoked thoughts of Bee.

"I'm Ara," she introduced herself. Her tourmaline skin and body language were soft and calm, while her expression showed confusion but her lips curved into a warm, genuine smile. There was an undeniable mix of shyness and appreciation, reminiscent of someone familiar.

"Have we met before?" Nick inquired, a sense of déjà vu passing over him.

"No," Ara replied softly, her voice quivering slightly with unspoken feelings.

"You don't know me, but I have an extraordinary creation of your mother's," he said, partially extending the Acme box toward her. The silky, polished aluminum device shone under the room's soft lighting; it had never looked so clean and new—now a symbol of hope and closure. Ara peered at the device. "This is Acme AI, or more precisely, Acme Amy, version 17.0. Your mother was the brilliant mind behind this exceptional software... before... she passed. It truly is groundbreaking."

Nick presented the small, unassuming unit, packed with all the potential, now fully stretched out before him. Relief washed over him as it was about to leave his hands—a burdensome secret exchanged for a shared purpose.

"You mean my aunt?" Ara asked, furrowing her brow.

Nick puckered in confusion, yet he pressed on, struggling to articulate the thoughts he'd rehearsed during his journey to meet her. "This… is her legacy," he uttered, his voice heavy with emotions he'd only now begun to confront. "Ehe, it helped me win the race."

"Nick, my mother is upstairs. Amy Spaceman is my aunt, and she's alive. She's in the Milky Way, searching for this Acme AI box."

"Ehe, I—I don't understand. I—" Nick found himself in a fountain of confusion and uncertainty. He was increasingly perplexed and bewildered.

"During the last interstellar video call with her, she thought she'd located this." Ara's eyes looked down at the box.

Nick nodded for her to continue and let out a shallow sigh, bracing himself to deduce her words.

"There was a black sportscar that belonged to her late boyfriend, who tragically perished in a house fire," she said. "She stored the Acme system inside the black car, which disappeared and was never seen again." She paused, but Nick said nothing, so she continued, "Over the years, she's been tracing it but only recently located both the car and its new owner in an old mining town on Planet Earth. On the outskirts of Las Vegas." Ara was equally baffled, her voice resonating flat as she un-trapped the enigma. She pieced together the mystery for both herself and Amy Spaceman.

"What kind of car?" Nick's voice trembled with emotion.

"I think she called it a—" She thought momentarily, "Porsh?"

"Ehe, Oh." He calmly gazed as if peering through her body or into outer space.

"Yes, I think that's what she said. She's been on Earth for seven years, Nick, trying to recover her technology. She traveled to Earth to escape Karl, who attempted to assault her for the new software. She hid it on Earth in a gentleman's car, her boyfriend or something, where she continued to test the software. She said an Earthling named Nick owned the car now." Ara finished to inhale. She had the puzzle clearly unraveled.

Nick's mouth fell open, his browline pressed together, and his eyes widened with surprise.

"At work, she even requested a change in her delivery route so she could spy on him and retrieve the box," Ara added questionably. "She tried to spy on him and even steal it, but she said he was a really nice guy."

Nick settled onto the lobby sofa, setting the Acme AI beside him with another sigh. He shielded his eyes with his hand and lowered his head, contemplating, lost in thought for a moment.

Ara began to elaborate, "She's a delivery driver. She's lived on Earth for years as a human guiser. She works delivering packages... and plays tennis." As she spoke, she shared her knowledge freely with him. "She mentioned that she plays tennis with the owner of the sportscar. She told me he was a really nice person... It was you."

Then Nick whispered under his breath, "Bee."

"What?" Ara whispered back.

"When did you last video call?" Nick's heart tightened as he recalled Bee's beautiful smile, the way she carried an air of optimism that seemed to pierce his often deep brooding. They'd shared simple moments—laughing about mundane things like the weather or her amusing delivery routes. He remembered the motion of her hand when she playfully mimicked his wrench moves and her inviting laughter during his tennis lessons. Those were the moments that made the alien weight on his shoulders feel lighter, if only for a while.

"Sometime last week. She was crying. She won the tennis match, Nick."

A sense of completion blossomed in Nick's chest as he envisioned Bee pulling on the glovebox latch of the Porsche.

He raised his hand skyward, palm open. "Don't tell me anymore." Standing tall, he grasped the Acme AI once again. With a heartfelt farewell to Ara, he turned away and departed.

He climbed back into his spacecraft, adjusting the tuning knobs in his ETV, his conversation with Ara serving as a comforting final note to F5. The thrumming hum of the engines began his departure, the stars beyond stretched invitingly.

As he lifted off, the buzzing city faded away into the backdrop, then the world faded, and then its sun faded into a star. His mind's eye flickered with images as he sliced through the heavens. Toward Earth, with new dreams and the residual echoes of old attachments, he went.

To be continued…

Thank you for enjoying Nick and the 996. If you enjoyed this book, kindly leave a 5-star review where you purchased.

www.ingramcontent.com/pod-product-compliance
Lightning Source LLC
Chambersburg PA
CBHW022215170626
46807CB00005B/2369